LIKE A ROARING LION

----------Book 1-----------

THE MARK OF THE BEAST

A Fiction Based on Ancient Manuscripts

E. LYE

While *Like a Roaring Lion* is fictitious in nature, it is based on several ancient manuscripts including the Bible, the book of Enoch, and the Dead Sea Scrolls. Names, characters, places, and incidents either are the product of the author's imagination or are used fictitiously. Any resemblance to actual persons, living or dead, events, or locales is entirely coincidental.

Published by SuburbanBuzz.com LLC

ISBN: 0-9896377-6-X
ISBN-13: 978-0-9896377-6-3

Dedication

To the Dream Maker,

While I slumber and cannot protest, you corrupt my mind with lies—with tales that never happened and places that don't exist.

> ...As the buildings crumble and the earth cracks, I hear Death call my name.
> ...As my outspread wings lift me over the treetops, the talons of my enemy sink into my back.
> ...From the dark closet, I see the fright in her wide eyes as the glass coffin fills with water.
> ...I answered the ringing phone, and it was the dead lady calling from Hell.

This tale will be told—elaborated, perhaps.
None the less, without you Dream Maker, it would not exist.

CONTENTS

Acknowledgments

I would like to express a deep appreciation to the beautiful and talented Holly Chervnsik who trimmed and polished my book into a Rembrandt. This remarkably talented lady completed the editing, text formatting, book cover design, and the publishing. Thank you for being kind and considerate while offering unprecedented skills.

Thank you to my son—my good and perfect gift from above. From the moment he came into existence, my life forever changed. I, at last, knew how deeply one could love. Feeling the love I have for my child has given me an idea of how God must love us, his children.

Thank you to my mom for being my number one fan. According to her, I'm the smartest person on the face of this planet. She gave me the attitude that I could do anything I set my heart on. Because of a life packed with support and encouragement of that magnitude, I'm inclined to believe that I can do just about anything—like write a book.

Thank you to my lifelong best friend for constant support. Her encouragement to consider the feelings of others and to treat everyone with respect regardless of their race, religion, or social status weighed heavy on my heart and my mind as I wrote the words of this book.

Thank you to all my Catholic friends and family for understanding and accepting that this book is not an attack against you or any member of the Catholic church. It does, however, state some ugly known facts about the establishment itself. Thank you for remembering that this is a book of fiction.

I always save the best for last. If I didn't say that, somebody (my dear spouse) would be greatly offended. Thank you from the bottom of my heart. If it weren't for you, there would be no book—for there would have been no time in which to have written a book. My and my son's life took a major turn for the better when we met you. You are full of love, kindness, and devotion for your family and friends. You have made my dreams come true, including finally finishing my first book.

Introduction

O nce again, Epic found himself soaring over the Serengeti region between Kenya and Tanzania, scavenging for easy prey. Since the rains had ceased and the streams had run dry, the great wildebeests had migrated off toward the north in search of food and water.

Below, Motak, in sandals and purple robe, had walked for twelve hours with his herd of cattle to drink from the crater along with the other herders and various wildlife. Like most other Maasi, he was lean from a scant diet and much walking. With his long spear in one hand and cow whistle in the other, he relentlessly led his beloved cattle closer to the life-giving pool.

As Epic flew over Motak, he saw his weakness and chose to take him as he reached the tourists that were gathered at the crater.

Motak, with his plaited hair adorned with shiny beads and his wooden earrings dangling from pendulous lobes, was now close enough to see the smiling tourists. Motak knew that he was a novelty to the fair skinned people. As he approached, he began proudly posing for the cameras. With a big grin on his face, he stood with chest out, chin up, and spear held up high for all to see.

At that very moment, Epic summoned Janna, the hungry lioness, to charge Motak. Janna sprinted from the waterhole. The tourists screamed and began running toward their tour bus. Motak turned to see why they were screaming. But it was too late. Janna sprang into the air, sunk her claws into Motak's back and her teeth into his neck, killing him instantly. As his life blood flowed out onto the brown dirt, from the windows of the bus, the tourists looked on in terror. But Janna paid them no mind as she proudly sauntered back to the waterhole.

Epic was gluttonous when it came to the Maasi people. That day alone, he had devoured twenty others before their souls could be lost.

Chapter 1
The Girl of My Dreams

Far, far away from the Serengeti, and possessing no knowledge of it, stirred Sam Webber. High on the cliff side, Sam awakened just in time to witness the beginning of another beautiful Saturday morning. As the sun began to peak over the horizon, its orange and yellow hues quickly took over the darkness of the night. He watched as the sun's beams spread out over the ocean, causing the colors of the sky and ocean to merge and appear as one. As Sam's eyes were captivated by the quickly changing colors of the sky, he opened his bedroom window so that the rest of his senses could feast on the delicacies of the morning. His ears eagerly received the sounds of the waves rhythmically crashing into the rocks below. Cool and refreshing was the summer breeze on his skin, and sweet was the aroma of the salty Oregon ocean.

As he looked out over the ocean, his mind wandered back to the night. He turned to look at the nearby lighthouse and tried to remember where its searchlight had traveled over the water - tried to remember where it was that he saw the winged creature flying just above the dark waves. It wasn't the first time that Sam thought he had seen it. The first time, he had called out for his parents to come and see. To Sam's disappointment, they didn't see a thing other than the rolling waves. The next morning, he and his parents searched the rocks below and didn't find anything conspicuous. As usual, they were kind with their remarks. They told Sam that anyone that stares out into the dark ocean for long periods of time would eventually see something that isn't there. "It's just your eyes playing tricks on you," they explained.

But Sam wasn't convinced they were correct. He spent hours, nearly every night, following the searchlight as it skimmed over the water. Sam couldn't count the number of times he had caught a glimpse of the dark creature. Maybe, he thought, it was the ghost of some shipwreck from long ago. Every night was an adventure as Sam waited and watched with binoculars in hand, while the sun allowed the night to take over.

As much as Sam admired the night for its dark mysteries, equally did he treasure the beautiful mornings. As the sun peaked over the horizon, erasing the night, he thought about how fortunate he was to live where he did. A school friend of his, Fred, lived in an apartment in town. Sam had slept over several times, and he and Fred stayed up into the wee hours of the morning playing video games. While he did have a great time at Fred's, he missed everything about his home on the coast in Tillamook, Oregon. It had been his only home since the day of his birth. Plus, his loving grandparents lived about a mile down the winding road, and he often walked to their house to visit.

Sunday was Sam's favorite day, since his grandmother, without fail, baked either an angel food cake, a German chocolate cake, or one of her delicious cream-filled pies. Always, over a piece of pie, Sam would tell his grandparents all about his latest mountain hiking adventure. He loved hiking in the nearby hills, as did his grandparents when they were younger. As his grandparents enthusiastically listened to their one and only grandchild, Grandpa chimed in with embellished stories of his younger days. When Sam thought his grandpa might be exaggerating a bit, he would look at his grandmother's expression. She would give him a roll of her eyes and a smile to let Sam know that Grandpa was, indeed, enriching the story.

Saturday nights were another favorite of Sam's. They were reserved for dominoes and cards at his grandparent's house. Three of his grandfather's best friends always met there and played games until midnight. Sometimes, they played a few games of Spades. When they did, Sam knew that there would be an uprising between Grandpa and Earl, his closest friend, because they were very competitive. One minute, there would be silence as they were studying their cards and devising their playing strategy. A few minutes later, somebody was raising their voice at somebody else for playing, what they considered to be, the wrong card. Sam had always been amused by the way they could raise Cain with each other yet depart with no ill feelings. At the stroke of midnight, they would all rise from the table, shake hands with a goodnight farewell, and depart as best friends. That scene always reminded Sam of the cartoon with Wile E. Coyote and Sam Sheepdog. In the cartoon, Sam Sheepdog and Wile E. Coyote would say good morning to each other as they punched in at the time clock. Sam Sheepdog's job was to protect the sheep. Opposing him, was Wile E. Coyote, whose job was to steal and eat the sheep. All day, they were on opposite sides. But at the end of the day, they were again cordial as they punched out at the time clock.

"Have a good afternoon, Sam," Wile E. Coyote would say.

"See you in the morning," Sam Sheepdog would mutter back.

It was the same with Grandpa and his friends. The only thing missing was the time clock.

Sam had fond memories of his grandparent's friends. They always made him feel like the life of the party. He never had to bring his own money to join the poker games, because they would each chip in and give Sam more than enough spare change to play with.

Beautiful scenery and plenty of love from his family were all that Sam knew. The only thing that he thought was missing from his life was a brother or a sister, and it was the one and only thing he intended to change when he had a family of his own. He planned on, one day, raising his children as he was raised—right there on the coast, close to his parents. He couldn't picture himself anywhere else.

"Family first," had been echoed in Sam's home since he was old enough to remember. As a family, they did everything together. One of their family's goals was to visit every lake in Oregon—which they did. At each Lake, they camped in a tent and ate the fish they caught from the lake. Hiking around the different lakes was always a new adventure with a surprise around each bend. Waterfalls were plentiful at some lakes, while ancient lava flows created magical landscapes at others. Crystal clear water, hot springs, and unimaginable natural wonders etched memories into each of their minds.

Sam knew he was fortunate to have the life that he did. He knew that many of his friends at school didn't share his good fortune. Several of which were from broken homes, and Sam could see sadness in their faces and hear insecurity in their voices. He knew that he was somehow different than them—better off than them.

The girls at school were a big mystery to Sam. He dated several, but couldn't find one that shared the same life goals and interest as his. Often, he voiced his concern about finding "the right girl" to his parents. His parents, Sam Sr. and Ruth, advised him to patiently wait because he was still young and had plenty of time. That conversation always ended with the same bit of advice. "When the right girl comes along, you'll know it." Believing them to be older and wiser, he cherished their advice. So, he dated around but waited for that feeling of knowing when that one and only "right girl" came along.

After he graduated from high school, his parents offered to pay for his college education. Gladly accepting, Sam followed in his Dad's footsteps and studied law. Attending the University of Oregon School of Law, he obtained his law degree. Being in a hurry to get on with his life, Sam worked diligently to finish as quickly as possible. He graduated with a law degree at twenty-six. His parents couldn't have been prouder of their one and only child. As far as they were concerned, Sam was the perfect son, and the sky was the limit for him.

Like most loving parents, they wanted badly for their son to be prosperous, as well as happy. They looked forward to the day when Sam would meet "the right girl." They were positive that Sam would choose the right one. After all, he had made all the right decisions thus far. His mother, Ruth, yearned for the day that he would give her grandchildren. She desired to be just like her mother and bake goodies for her grandchildren every weekend. In her mind, they would all be one big happy family, living right next to each other on the coast. In fact, they planned on giving Sam the acre next to theirs, on which to build his home.

Upon Sam's graduation, Sam Sr. and Ruth threw a big celebration at their house on the coast for Sam. Friends came, and they brought their friends who brought their friends. In all, two hundred and eighty people attended Sam's graduation party. They were spread all over the lawn and all through the house. They sat on the cliff's edge and on the patio around the fire pit.

Since Sam had been raised with manners, he diligently tried to make his way around to visit and thank everyone for coming. As he walked across the lawn, toward the edge of the cliff, something shiny caught his eye. He turned to see what it was and saw that it was a girl's shiny black hair dancing in the wind. The sun had hit it just right so that it radiated through the whole crowd all the way back to Sam, reminding him of the spotlight on the lighthouse. He stopped for a while and leaned against the old oak tree that his parents had carved their initials into years before when they first purchased the property. He watched as the girl talked to her friends, with her long black hair still fluttering in the breeze. Intrigued by her beauty, he knew he had to meet her. He began to walk in her direction.

The voices in Staci's head said, "He's the one." She turned just in time to see him approaching. He was looking directly at her.

"Sam, my man, great party!" said Fred, Sam's longtime friend.

"Oh, yeah, thank my parents. They did everything. All I did was show up," he laughed as he noticed the girl with the long hair was looking directly at him.

"Are you going to introduce me to your friends?" Sam asked.

"Oh, yeah, what's wrong with me?" chuckled Fred.

Sam was introduced to practically the whole group of about fifteen before he finally had the pleasure of meeting her.

"And this beauty is Staci," said Fred.

Smiling, Staci reached her hand out as Sam took it, turned it over, kissed the back side of it, and said, "Very nice to meet you."

Seductively, she smiled and replied, "Nice to meet you too. I've heard lots of great things about you from Fred."

"Oh no, not everyone knows this, but my friend, Fred here, has a contagious disease known as F.O.S. I don't mean to alarm you, but since you're here for my party, I feel responsible for getting you away from him as soon as possible. I can take you on a tour of the place while you tell me everything he said. I'll let you know if it's true or not," Sam joked as everyone laughed.

"Talk about F.O.S., I believe that you had an agenda when you walked over here," laughed Fred. "You're not falling for that line of crap, are you Staci?" asked Fred.

"Why not? It's well constructed. I believe it's the best line I've ever heard," sweetly answered Staci.

Sam held out his arm for Staci to grab on to and said, "Very well then. First, let me show you to my bedroom." Everyone laughed, including Staci. Sam was always funny, very seldom serious, and kept his friends and family laughing and smiling.

The two walked toward the edge of the cliff, where they sat and talked until late in the evening after most of the others had gone home.

"Where are you from?" asked Sam.

"Roseburg, near the border of California."

"That explains it. I've always heard that there are beautiful women down there, and you are the most beautiful I've ever seen."

"Thank you," she said as she gave him a small kiss on the cheek and quickly retreated back. That one small kiss sent Sam's heart reeling, as she knew it would. She had always been beautiful and knew exactly how to use it to her advantage. Staci could see that Sam was very attracted to her, and she could also see the big spread that his parents owned. Knowing that Sam had just graduated from law school, she knew that he would make the kind of money she was interested in. He was exactly what she had been waiting for—not only a man that adored her and would give her anything her heart desired, but one that could afford it.

She was glad that the voices agreed.

When she saw the look in Sam's eyes after that one small kiss on his cheek, she knew her search was over. She was ready to drop out of college and be taken care of in the manner she knew she deserved.

To Sam, the small kiss on the cheek was just an invitation for a more seductive kiss. Without hesitation, he turned toward her and leaned in closer while looking into her eyes. Testing her reaction, Sam began with just a quick kiss on the lips, which led to another and then another. Wanting to make herself completely irresistible to Sam, Staci began to nibble on Sam's bottom lip, then seductively thrust her tongue into his mouth. She knew exactly what Sam was thinking of at that very moment. Her grand finale consisted of sucking and licking his neck then kissing and nibbling on his chin. He had been with a lot of college girls and to a lot of college parties, but no girl had made him feel quite like Staci did. His primitive instincts were aroused, and all he could think about was taking her to his bedroom and having his way with her. But he knew he should, instead, quickly change the mood. He knew he couldn't take another kiss like that and remain a gentleman.

By the looks of his bulging pants, Staci knew she had succeeded.

"Where have you been all my life?" he asked.

"Down South," she smiled.

"By the way, what brings you up here?"

She turned, looked back at her group of friends, and said, "Do you see that girl with the red dress and short blond hair? She's my dorm mate. She's dating your friend, Fred, and they invited me to come along."

"Well, I'm glad you accepted. Are you getting cold?" he asked when he noticed she was rubbing her arms.

"Yes, a little."

"Let's go up to the fire pit and get you warmed up."

Once to the fire pit, Sam stated, "Tell me a little about your family."

She awkwardly looked out into the darkness and answered, "There's really not much to tell. I'm adopted, and I'm not very close to them. They financially support me while I'm going to college, which I'm very grateful for, but we never really bonded. Probably because I was already twelve years old when they adopted me."

"I'm so sorry to hear that. If you don't mind me asking, what happen to your biological parents?"

Still looking into the darkness and away from Sam, Staci answered, "They were actually murdered. Someone broke into our lake house, found my Dad's gun, and shot both him and my mother to death."

"Oh, my God! Where were you?"

Quickly, she turned and looked into the fire as she answered, "I was asleep in my bed. Luckily, they didn't come to my room. When I woke up in the morning, I found them both dead, lying in their bed. They were both shot in the head."

Sam thought it strange the way she told the story so nonchalantly, but her beauty and seductive kiss excused her.

"That's horrible! That must have messed you up for a while."

With an expressionless gaze, Staci looked at Sam and responded, "I was sent to counseling for many years. It must have helped because I feel fine now."

"I'm glad to hear that. Would you like another drink?" he asked, wanting to escape the eerie feeling of the subject he embarked on.

"I would love one," she smiled, also wanting to leave that subject.

After a couple more drinks, they talked late into the night about their life dreams and goals. Of course, Staci didn't tell Sam that hers was to find a wealthy man to seduce into giving her everything she wished for.

Sam told her that he wanted a family, a big family, with lots of kids since he was an only child. He dreamed of Christmas holidays with his parents, he and his wife, and his children all gathered together for a big feast. Knowing that his parents wanted grandchildren, especially a granddaughter, he wanted to live within walking distance from them. He told Staci how he always walked to his grandparent's house, about his grandmother's yummy desserts, domino night, and how much he adored living near them. He told her he also loved the coast and wanted to remain nearby. Staci heard the words coming from his mouth, but did not care what he wanted. She only pretended to care. Not until the sun began to rise, did Sam realize they had visited all night long.

The two became inseparable. They dated for one year and then married. They rented a small apartment, not far from Sam's parents, until they decided where they would settle. As previously decided, Sam's parents offered the young couple one of their acres, but Staci insisted that they wait before making a decision which affected both of them. Highly disappointed, Sam Sr. and Ruth knew that their hands were tied, and all they could do was hope and pray that Staci would change her mind.

One afternoon when Sam came home to visit, his parents expressed their concerns to him.

Pleasantly smiling, Ruth stated, "We can see that you really love Staci a lot. We like her too, but she is so quiet around us that we aren't sure if she likes us."

Sam Sr. wasn't as sensitive and nurturing as Ruth. He flat out stated how he really felt. "Son, I highly respect you, but I feel that Staci has seduced you with her good looks and charms. I'm concerned that your best interest is not her priority. And, she's so quiet around us that I can't help but believe she's hiding something. It's as if she doesn't want to let us know who she really is. I don't want to offend you, but I'm really concerned."

"You're not offending me, Dad. I know y'all want the best for me. You're right! She is quiet around you and Mom, but I think I know why. You see, she went through a terrible tragedy as a young child that I think still greatly affects her. I probably should have told you in the beginning, but I didn't want to worry you," explained Sam.

"Oh, well, what happened?" sweetly asked Ruth.

"I have to warn you; it's a pretty frightening story. So here goes. When she was a little girl, she and her parents were at their lake house. And, one night, while she was asleep in her bedroom, someone broke in, found her Dad's gun, and shot both of her parents in the head while they slept."

"What? Oh, my God! That is horrible," squealed Ruth.

Sam continued on, "After her parents were murdered, she was adopted. She never really got close to her adopted parents. So I think that she doesn't really know how to be close to you since she didn't have that as a child. Do you know what I mean?"

As his mother sat wide-eyed and speechless, again, not beating around the bush, his dad asked, "Did they ever find the killer?"

"No, they never did," Sam answered.

"How old was Staci, and where did you say she was?" he continued.

"She was only eleven, and she was asleep in her bedroom," Sam answered.

"Did she hear the gunshots?" his father inquired.

"I've never asked her that, but she must not have. She didn't find out they had been shot until morning when she found them in their bed," Sam answered with a puzzled look on his face, as though he had never thought about that before.

"Oh, my God!" repeated his mother. "That's probably exactly why she is distant to us. That's horrible! She lost her parents at such a young age. And, she wasn't really close to anyone growing up, so she just doesn't know how."

Once their son left, Sam Sr. asked Ruth, "Is it just me, or isn't it awfully suspicious that Staci was in the house when her parents were shot and never heard gunfire?"

"Oh, Sam, she was only eleven. Surely, you are not suspicious that she shot her own parents at eleven years old?" she asked, frowning at him with disapproval.

"I know it sounds farfetched, but how could she not hear gunfire in the house?"

"I don't know. Maybe, since she was so young, she slept very deeply and didn't hear it. Besides, I'm sure there was an investigation. If she had shot them, the police surely would have found out."

"I guess you're right," he gave in, realizing he could not break through Ruth's protective mothering instincts.

Regardless of Staci's strange behavior, Sam's parents hoped that the two wouldn't move far away from them.

But just as they feared, Staci chose a house far away in Klamath Falls, Oregon, near Crater Lake. It was a beautiful drive through the quiet forest of hemlocks but took several hours for Sam's parents to drive the long distance from their coastal home in Tillamook.

On their first drive, Sam Sr. asked Ruth, "I know this may be stretching it a bit, but you don't think that Crater Lake is the lake where Staci's parents were murdered, do you?"

"Oh, I don't think Staci would want to live anywhere near the same lake where her parents were murdered," she answered.

"That would be very strange," he stated.

"Please don't ask her, Sam. We have to be polite for Sam's sake," she said as she studied his facial expressions.

"What makes you think I want to ask her?" he said with a smirky grin.

"I've known you practically my whole life. I always know what you're thinking," she answered as she lovingly patted his leg.

Once they arrived, Sam gave his parents a tour of the house.

Then the two couples sat in the living room drinking coffee and visiting with each other. They talked about how pretty the house was, how pretty the scenery was, the temperature, the neighborhood, how pretty their new furniture was, and all about their recent honeymoon to Cancun.

Sam Sr. thought he had waited long enough to ask, and so he began in a roundabout way.

"How far is the lake from here, Staci?"

"Oh, it's about an hour and a half away," she answered.

"Is it a nice lake?" he continued, even though he could see his wife sternly staring at him from the corner of his eye.

"Oh, it's beautiful most of the time. But sometimes, during the winter, there's so much snow, you can't get to it."

"Sounds like you've been there often," he said as he refused to look in his wife's direction.

"Yes, I went there often as a child," she answered unwaveringly.

Ruth knew what the next question would be, and so she intervened.

"Is anyone hungry?"

Sam knew where his dad was going with the conversation, as well, and sided with his mom. "Yes, we were waiting for you guys to get here before we ate. There's a great restaurant in town I'd like to take you to."

"Well, let's load up and go," his mom cheerfully agreed.

Sam Sr. wasn't going to let them sabotage his conversation.

"Is that where your family's lake house was?" he asked as everyone was getting up to leave.

Staci stopped dead in her tracks. Surprised that he had the boldness to ask, she glared at him as if it were none of his business.

Even though Sam and Ruth opposed the questioning, they were

14

both also curious. They stopped walking toward the door and turned to observe Staci's response. Not even her new husband, Sam Jr., knew the answer.

"Yes, it is. But I don't like to talk about it," she responded as she swirled around so quickly that it caused her long black hair to whip upward. As Staci walked toward the front door, Sam Sr., Ruth, and Sam were all looking into each other's faces with daunting expressions.

The rest of the evening, Staci hardly spoke a word. She was obviously perturbed at Sam Sr. for asking such a question.

Sam was surprised that his new wife hadn't told him that they were living near the lake house in which her parents were murdered. They were all shocked and weren't sure what to think about her curious behavior. Sam had seen how she reacted to his dad for asking, so, he decided to let it go and continue the conversation sometime down the road.

Klamath Falls was a much colder climate than Sam's coastal childhood home, so he very much enjoyed going back home to visit his family.

At first, Sam made sure he and Staci went home to visit every two weeks. After their first born, Andrew, arrived, their visits were cut to once a month. Then, three years later, when Elizabeth was born, they were only able to visit every three to four months. During the long spans away from home, Sam would often telephone his parents and talk for quite a while. They could hear in Sam's voice that he missed them and had grown homesick.

It seemed to his parents that Staci had purposely weaned Sam from them. When Sam and Staci did visit his parents, Staci sat on the couch quietly while Sam and his parents played with the two children. It was obvious to the whole family that she didn't want to be there. Having respect for marriage and for Sam, Sam Sr. and Ruth couldn't express their worries to their son. But once the two were alone, they would openly discuss their worries about Staci. When they visited the young couple, Sam Sr. and Ruth could tell that their once happy son was not emotionally well. But their hands were tied. They didn't know how to help Sam.

Chapter 2
September 7, 2011
Son of Sam

Ryan Hucklby lived across the street from Andrew Webber, and they were very best friends. Both of them had lived there on Trippell St. since they were born, and had known each other their whole lives. They were so young when they started playing together that they couldn't even remember how they met. As soon as Ryan got off of the school bus each day, he would run into the house to let his mom know he was home. Then, he would run across the street to play with Andrew, who was always inside waiting for him. Andrew didn't go to the public school because he was homeschooled by his mom, Staci Webber.

Ryan knew to quietly knock on the front door, as Ms. Staci instructed. Andrew was careful not to run, but to walk to answer the door, or else his mother would ground him again. Once outside, they would run through the forest behind Andrew's house, hiding behind trees, and pretend shooting each other. If they were not playing war, they were playing football or baseball. In the winter months, they played in the snow making snow people and sledding down the hills around their houses.

On the ground, right outside of Andrew's bedroom window, was a large stump from an old oak tree that had been cut down. With it, the two boys could easily climb in and out of the window, which they did on numerous occasions, especially at night. "Hide-and-go-seek" was more fun at night. Of course, they knew they were taking a big chance. They had been caught once before, and Andrew was grounded for two days because of it. During the grounding, they missed each other terribly, and the two days seemed like an eternity.

They were the same age with their birthdays only two weeks apart from each other. Both were born in September, and both were ten years old. Each had light brown hair and were about the same height. They had so much in common and were so close that they felt like real brothers. In fact, when they would meet someone new in the neighborhood, Andrew would say, "Hi, I'm Andrew, and this is my soul brother, Ryan."

There wasn't a neighbor on the whole street that didn't know the two boys as soul brothers. All the neighbors also knew Andrew's dad, Sam Webber and Andrew's little sister, Elizabeth. Andrew's dad and sister went for walks with the soul brothers in the afternoon when Staci would nap or go to the grocery store. Staci never went for a walk. In fact, none of the neighbors had ever talked to or knew Staci. They barely knew what she looked like. The only time they saw her was when she came outside to call the kids in for the afternoon or when she was in her car attending errands. She wouldn't let the children have bikes because she didn't want them too far away. If they were not within ear range when she called from the door, they were grounded for a couple of days.

When the weekend rolled around, Ryan knew to wait for Andrew to telephone to say he was finished with his chores before going over to play.

One dreaded Saturday, Ryan didn't hear from Andrew at all. He figured that Andrew was either sick or grounded for something. He called him on the phone, but there was no answer. So, that afternoon, Ryan decided to sneak over to Andrew's room for a visit. He climbed the fence with the help of another old stump that often assisted the two boys in sneaking in and out of Andrew's yard. As the sun was sinking below the distant mountains, Ryan crept silently along the side of Andrew's house then ducked under the window of the living room as he made his way to the back of the house.

Trying not to make any noise that Andrew's mom would hear,

Ryan quietly climbed onto the stump near Andrew's bedroom window and cupped his hands around his eyes. He peered through the darkness into Andrew's bedroom and quietly muttered to himself, "Hmm! He usually watches TV when he's grounded."

It was so dark inside; he couldn't make anything out. Knowing that Andrew unlocked the window so that he could come in any time, Ryan slid it open and whispered, "Andrew, are you in here?"

Ryan heard no response, so he slid the window shut and crept silently back the way he came. Something hadn't felt right to Ryan. The house was too quiet and creepy. All day Sunday, Ryan worried about Andrew and watched his house. He detected no movement all day and thought that maybe the Webber's went to Oregon to visit the grandparents. All the next day at school, he wondered and worried if Andrew was all right. While the teacher talked about subjects and predicates, Ryan made plans to look into Andrew's window, only this time while it was still daylight.

The time dragged by ever so slowly as Ryan watched the clock on the wall. Finally, the school bell rang as the clock struck 3:00. Ryan made his way to the bus and was soon on his way home. The closer the bus got to Trippell Street, the more nervous Ryan became. As the bus passed by the front of Andrew's house, Ryan noticed that Staci's car was not in their driveway. Ryan knew that no one else drove her car and was relieved to see that she was not at home. The school bus came to a stop in front of Ryan's house. As soon as he stepped off of the bus, he went straight over the fence, climbed onto the stump, and peered into Andrew's window again. It was much brighter now, and he could see clearly inside. He didn't see Andrew but did see a red stain across the carpet.

"Oh, no! He must have spilled something," Ryan whispered to himself. "He probably got grounded again."

Carefully and quietly sliding the window open, he whispered, "Andrew."

Again, there was no response. He stayed there for several minutes, staring at the red stain, trying to figure out what Andrew had spilled. He noticed that the stain went all the way into the hall.

Although Ryan was scared of Mrs. Staci and scared of being caught by her, he climbed through the window anyway.

"Andrew must be in a lot of trouble. That's a big stain."

Ryan climbed onto the chest of drawers that aided them in and out of the window. As he did, one of Andrew's model trains fell off the top of the dresser, crashed to the floor, and broke the dead silence. He froze. He thought for sure that he would be caught. But nothing followed. No one came down the hall to find out what caused the noise.

No one asked, "Who's there?" In fact, there were no noises at all, just dead silence. It was such an eerie silence that goosebumps ran up and down Ryan's spine and arms. He rubbed his arms as he leaned closer to inspect the red stain on the tan carpet. Trying to figure out what it was, he followed it toward Andrew's bedroom door. He carefully peeked out into the hall. No one was there. The red stain was lighter, but there, as well. He followed it down the hall, where it became smaller and smaller. It went all the way into the garage.

"Maybe it's paint from one of Andrew's model trains," whispered Ryan to himself.

On the way back to Andrew's room, he passed Elizabeth's room. There was a red trail coming from her room, as well. Her bedroom door was cracked open. Fearing someone might be asleep in there, he very carefully pushed it open further. As his eyes fell on the bed, he saw the red stain on her bed too.

"What the heck?" he whispered and walked toward her bed. It was all over the pillow, the bed, and the floor. Ryan touched it with the tip of his pointer finger to see if it felt or smelled like paint. Once he felt the tacky substance, he realized it wasn't paint at all.

"That's blood," Ryan said louder than he meant to. His own voice startled him. With eyes wide as saucers, he quickly began backing out of Elizabeth's room. All the way, his eyes were locked on her blood-soaked pillow.

Once he had backed himself into the hallway, he ran back into Andrew's room and whispered, "This is a trail of blood." Panic struck him. Stumbling backward in fear, he found himself in the hall again. He looked down one end of the hall and then the other, terrified he would see Ms. Staci. Without thinking, he began running toward the front door. But the terror of running into a murderer changed his direction. Quickly, he ran back to Andrew's bedroom. Once there, he looked at Andrew's bed that he hadn't earlier. Ryan saw the same red stain on Andrew's pillow. He screamed, scaring himself even more. He tried to climb onto the dresser, stumbling and slipping several times before he could scale it. He sprang out of the window. Avoiding the stump, he crashed to his knees onto the leaf-covered ground next to it. Quickly recovering, he darted to his house across the street. As he was running through the front door, he was screaming, "Mom! Mom! Mom! Mom!"

"What?" Janice answered as she ran into the living room with wet hands from washing dishes.

Ryan ran straight into her and said, "Something bad happened to Andrew. There's blood everywhere."

"Where is there blood?" Janice asked as Ryan wrapped his arms around her waist. She could feel that he was shaking like a leaf.

"Everywhere in his room. In the hall. In Elizabeth's room. In the garage."

"Okay, calm down! Maybe it's something else. I'll have your dad go over there," she replied.

"No!" he said, shaking his head violently. "Call the police right now," he said with conviction.

Having never heard her son sound so distraught, Janice immediately picked up the phone and called the local police. Ryan wept the entire fifteen minutes it took the police to arrive. As the authorities went into Andrew's house, Ryan and his family watched from their front porch. Thirty minutes more, they heard more sirens coming toward them. That's when Ryan's parents, Janice and Alex, looked at each other and knew that something terrible did indeed happen to their neighbors across the street. Ryan began sobbing again and anchored his arms tightly around his mother. This time, she didn't tell him to calm down. She realized that her son was right all along. As the sun began to sink into the horizon, Trippell Street was ablaze with the flashing lights of all the emergency vehicles.

Chapter 3
Missing

An entire family was missing. The only evidence of a crime was blood scattered throughout the house. There was no murder weapon found, and no evidence of a break-in. Nothing of value was broken, destroyed, or seemed to be missing.

The local police went door to door asking the neighbors if they had seen anyone suspicious in the neighborhood. They all thought it, but no one would say that the mother might be the culprit. After all, they had no evidence, just gut feelings. For years, they had watched as Staci isolated herself and controlled every aspect of her family's lives. They had all thought she seemed a little strange.

Police Chief John Mitchell spotted Ryan sitting on his porch with his chin perched on his knees. Seeing Ryan reminded the chief of the first time he met the two boys. He had gone to visit his younger sister, who had just married and moved into a new house on Trippell Street. As the chief slowly drove down the street looking for his sister's car, Andrew and Ryan had excitedly run up to the open window and gleefully asked if they could sit in his patrol car and turn on the sirens. Chief Mitchell loved children and happily agreed. From that time forward, every time the boys would see the chief drive into the neighborhood, they would chase him down until his car came to a stop in front of his sister's house. Each time, they would plead for a story about chasing bad guys and ask to flip the switch for the sirens. There was no way the chief could say no to them. He had just as much fun with the two boys as they did with him.

The chief walked up to Ryan, shook his hand, and said, "Hey

buddy, how are you doing?"

"Okay," is all Ryan said as he continued looking downward.

"I understand that you went to pay Andrew a visit today."

"Yes, sir, but I didn't do anything," he answered with guilt that stemmed from sneaking through the window.

"Don't worry Buddy. You didn't do anything wrong. I just want you to tell me what you saw."

Ryan told the chief everything and then had to retell the story to several other officials.

The chief knew that he had a good rapport with Ryan, so he walked him a few feet away from the others and asked, "Between me and you, what do you think may have happened here?"

"I think it was Andrew's mom," frankly stated Ryan as he looked right into the police chief's eyes. The chief was puzzled as Ryan spoke. Impulsively, the chief assumed that Ryan was just a kid with a childish imagination. But he didn't want Ryan to know he thought so.

"Well, Buddy, what makes you think that it was his mom?"

"I don't know."

"Did she ever hurt Andrew?"

"No, she's just mean."

"Okay, I'm going to look into that. I trust your judgment, and I want to thank you for all of your help. I'm going to do everything I can do to find your friend. You've been very brave," he added as he hugged Ryan tightly. With his arm draped around Ryan's shoulders, he walked the boy back to his parents.

The chief took Janice and Albert aside and explained how detrimental it could be for a child to see a bloody crime scene. He strongly suggested they seek counseling for Ryan right away.

As the sky darkened, many of the emergency vehicles began to drive away. Ryan and his parents slowly made their way back to their house.

After a couple of hours, the loud roaring of the helicopters could be heard overhead, which made Ryan's stomach churn. Every once in a while, one of the bright search beams would radiate through their living room and illuminate Ryan's teary eyes. Janice sat on the couch with Ryan and tried to console him. But there was no convincing him that things would ever be all right again. Deep within his soul, he knew he would never again see his soul brother alive.

The whirling of the helicopter blades became fainter as the search got wider and further away. Ryan's mother watched him rise from the couch, where he had been for hours, and peer through the window with his hands cupped around his eyes.

"They're looking in the mountains now," he quietly muttered.

His mom got up and stood beside him. She could see the bright beams slicing through the darkness into the Cascade Mountains that sat to the west.

"I know it was his mom," Ryan said.

"We have to wait and see, Honey," answered Janice.

"No one believes me," he cried and ran into his bedroom, shutting and locking the door behind him.

Janice looked at Alex and began sobbing, "Why did he lock his door?"

Ground search and rescue teams were called in the next day. After searching for one week, not a shred of evidence was found. The teams became smaller as the days went by. After two weeks, the search was called off. The area around their neighborhood was vast, and there were thick woods and rocky cliffs, which made searching difficult.

Alex and Janice decided to form a neighborhood search team of their own. Sam's parents joined in along with many of Sam's old classmates and friends, including Fred. Several citizens of Klamath also joined the search.

As they began the search, several of the locals muttered, "Nothing like this has ever happened here before."

The community had been a quiet and safe place for as long as they could remember. Now, they no longer felt safe in their own homes.

Sam's parents didn't speak it to anyone, but in the back of their minds, they shared Ryan's fear. So, after a day of searching the area, Sam Sr. and Ruth decided to visit the local police department.

"Pleased to meet you, folks. I can't tell you how sorry I am, but I can assure you that I will do everything within my power to solve this," said Chief John Mitchell.

"Thank you! We just wanted to come down here to let you know something about Staci, our son's wife. We think it may be pertinent to the case," Sam Sr. announced.

"Oh, yes, please, any time you can think of anything that may help, no matter how insignificant you think it may be, please don't hesitate to let me know."

"Thank you! We'll keep that in mind. What we wanted to tell you was that Staci once told Sam, our son, that her parents were killed in their lake house when she was only eleven. Apparently, they were both shot in the head while they slept. Staci claimed that she was asleep in her room and never heard anything, and then she found them both dead in the morning. She was the only one alive in the house. And, if that's not weird enough, she moved herself and my son into a house close to that same lake and never bothered letting our son know that it was the same lake," continued Sam Sr.

"Wow! You mean the house on Trippell St.?" the chief asked.

"Yes," Sam Sr. answered.

"That's very odd. The whole incident raises red flags. And, it's pretty unbelievable that she wouldn't have heard gunfire. Do you know where the lake house in which her parents were murdered in is located?"

"All I know is that it's somewhere close to Crater Lake,"

"I'm glad you let me know this information. I'll send a crew out to search around the lake just in case. Do you know what happened to Staci after her parents were murdered?"

"She was adopted after that and raised in Roseburg," added Ruth.

"Do you know if there was an investigation linking her to the crime?"

"Unfortunately, we never looked into that. So no, we don't know," Sam Sr. said with a disappointing sigh. He always had a gut feeling and would now have to live with the guilt of never checking further into it.

"Thank you for letting me know. I'm definitely going to look into this right away. Do you happen to know Staci's adopted last name?"

"She said it was Blake," answered Sam Sr.

As soon as they left the station, Chief Mitchell called the police chief of Roseburg to see if he knew anything about a Staci Blake.

"Oh, yes, we know of Staci Blake. She's a strange one, always has been."

"Can you give me some specifics on her," asked Chief Mitchell.

"Be glad to if you, in return, will tell me what she has done now," responded Chief Jackson.

"Deal," answered Chief Mitchell.

"I'll start from the beginning. The Blakes adopted her after her parents' mysterious murders. They must have called, oh, I don't know, five or six times to report her missing. Sometimes, she wouldn't make it home from school. She liked to run away to the woods. We would search for her until we found her and take her back home. All the way home, she talked to herself, but not to us. When we got her home, the Blakes always hugged her and acted real happy to have her back. They were real good people, and they had the patience of Job with that girl."

"Do you know if her parent's murders were ever solved?" asked Chief Mitchell.

"Nope, we had our suspicions, but no proof."

"Who did you suspect?"

"We were shunned so badly by the community when it got out that I almost don't like to tell anyone, but I'll tell you. We suspected Staci. She was an adorable eleven-year-old little girl that everybody felt sorry for. She cried at all the right times and looked real cute at other times. No one believed that a cute little girl like that could have ever killed her own parents. The gun that was registered to her dad, the one that we suspect killed them, disappeared. It's never been found. And the fact that she was the only other one in the house when they were shot, but swears that she didn't hear gunfire, is completely ridiculous. Nothing was stolen from the house either. No evidence of a break-in. Nothing was overturned. Three people in the house and two of them shot dead. Call me crazy, but that only leaves one possibility. I don't care how cute she was or is."

"You said she talked to herself?" inquired Chief Mitchell.

"Well, I say to herself. It actually always sounded like she was having a conversation with an imaginary friend. She would say stuff like, 'I told you he would find us there. Next time we'll go where I say.' She always made me feel like I had two people in the backseat," he chuckled.

"I may be calling you back for more info if you don't mind."

"Anytime," responded Chief Jackson.

"Thanks for your time," concluded Chief Mitchell.

"Not so fast. Remember, we had a deal," reminded Chief Jackson.

"Well, as of right now, she, her husband, and two children are missing. I was called out to their house two weeks ago and found a bloodbath. Her name keeps popping up. Many people seem to be suspicious of her," Chief Jackson replied.

"I'd bet my right one it was her," stated Chief Jackson.

"Hmm! So says everyone else. Well, thanks again for your time and information," said Chief Mitchell ending their conversation.

The small aircrew that Chief Mitchell sent out to Crater Lake found nothing conspicuous. The neighborhood search team continued for another week, and they found nothing. The area was so vast that everyone knew they would have to wait for a break in the case before the family would be found—if they ever were.

⋙⋘

Winter arrived quickly that year. As the yellow crime tape around Andrews's house started falling to the ground, the beautiful white snow completely covered it. But when spring arrived, and the snow melted, the yellow tape reappeared. It reminded all that saw it that an evil presence was still hiding somewhere in the midst. No one would remove the yellow tape. It became part of the vigil, even though life had to go on in Klamath Falls.

Children still went to school and adults went to work. Winter came and left again. Then spring and summer came and left again. And another winter came, and nothing changed. It was as though the Webber family had never existed.

Three years went by, and not a trace of evidence was discovered. No fingerprints, no forced entry, no murder weapon, and no evidence of any kind had been discovered. The blood spread throughout the house continued to be the only evidence that a crime was ever committed.

Ryan saw Chief Mitchell drive by slowly scanning the neighborhood at least once a week. He waved as he drove by, but he seldom stopped to talk to Ryan. Ryan figured it was because he felt bad and was embarrassed about not being able to find his friend, Andrew.

Meantime, Ryan and his family had been seeing a counselor once a week. It helped his family understand how Ryan felt. It also helped reassure Ryan that the same thing wouldn't happen to his family.

However, it couldn't make Ryan feel better about losing his very best friend. It didn't make Ryan stop having nightmares about Andrew's mom lurking in the darkness, waiting for her chance to kill everyone else in the neighborhood. He knew deep down in his soul that Staci Webber was somewhere out there, so he continued watching Andrew's house and all the surroundings. Before going to bed each and every night, he checked every window lock in the house and double checked the doors.

Chapter 4
Three Years Later

In the Klamath police station, there were two large boards on the wall opposite the counter; one with pictures of missing people and one with pictures of wanted criminals. It was purposely positioned there. That way, when someone approached the counter, they could quickly and inconspicuously be compared to the photographs on the board directly behind them. The missing included photos of Sam Webber, Staci Webber, Andrew Webber, and Elizabeth Webber. Also included was the date that they went missing in bold, black numbers. All of the officers were taught by Chief Mitchell to glance at the posters at the beginning of each shift so they would not be forgotten and always be fresh in their minds.

At 11 a.m. on the morning of September 7, 2014, a lady with long, dark, shiny hair walked up to the counter and asked, "May I please speak to Chief Mitchell?"

As usual for Klamath police department, it was a quiet day, so everyone looked up to see who was speaking.

She looked exactly as she looked in the portrait on the wall.

Nothing had changed. Her hair was exactly as it was in the photo on the board behind her.

Staci enjoyed watching as mouths fell open and pens dropped out of hands. No one had to call Chief Mitchell. Behind the glass wall of his office, he saw and heard her ask for him by name.

"Send her in," is all he said.

No one moved for several stunned seconds. Finally, the front desk clerk, sitting directly in front of her said, "This way, ma'am," and led her to the chief's office on the other side of the counter. As she walked through the maze of desks, no one spoke, just stared. Once she was behind closed doors with the chief, several of them whispered, "Isn't that the lady up there on that poster? I thought she was dead."

Chief Mitchell was already standing when she was escorted into his office. He pulled out the chair on the other side of his desk and motioned for her to sit down. He knew exactly who she was, but waited for her to tell him.

"How can I help you, ma'am?"

With a direct and stern look, she answered, "Do you not know who I am?"

"I was hoping you could tell me in case my inclination is wrong."

"You're not wrong. I'm Staci Webber."

He was hoping she would continue on, but she didn't. She just stared directly at him, waiting for his response.

"Mrs. Webber, you and your family have been missing for three years. I was at your home three years ago today. Do you know where your family is?"

"Do you mean, do I know where their bodies are buried?"

Cold chills ran down his spine as he recalled what Ryan and the grandparents had said about her. He had doubted it, but now knew how wrong he was.

"Ma'am, I'm going to inform you that our remaining conversation will be recorded, and I'm going to call another police officer in here, as well." He yelled out of his office door, "Jackson, come in here."

Jackson and the others had been eavesdropping, and they heard exactly what she had said.

He came in silently and stood by the door.

She looked back at him and said, "Don't worry. I have no intention of trying to escape."

Jackson didn't respond or change his stoic facial expression as he guarded her.

The chief pushed the record switch to on and said, "Ma'am, can you state your name for the record?"

"My name is Staci Webber."

"Why did you come in today?"

"To tell you where the bodies of Sam, Andrew, and Elizabeth are buried, and to turn myself in," she boldly stated with no remorse.

"Do you know where their bodies are located?"

"Yes, I do," she answered and stopped short of telling him where.

Annoyed at her, he asked, "You want to tell me where?"

"That's why I'm here," brashly, she answered.

"Ma'am, where are they?" He said with a raised voice.

"I buried them close to Crater lake," she answered.

He quickly recalled the conversation he had with the grandparents about Crater Lake and asked, "The same lake where your parents were murdered?"

Obviously aggravated at his question, she stood up and answered sternly, "Yes, but that has nothing to do with this."

Jackson shifted his body off of the door jam and instinctively put his hand on his gun.

"Please sit down, ma'am," calmly requested the chief.

After she sat down, the chief asked, "Mrs. Webber, did you murder your family?"

"Are you speaking of my parents, or my husband and children?"

"Right now, let's focus on your husband and children."

"I wouldn't say murdered. I graciously put them to rest. They didn't feel a thing. You must understand. I have business to attend to, and I must leave. I couldn't just leave them behind."

Her answer caused the chief to have so many questions that he wasn't sure which to ask first.

"So, where do you plan on going?"

"It's complicated. You wouldn't understand or believe me."

"Please, tell me anyway."

"If you insist. But don't say I didn't warn you. I've been called upon to help complete the mission of Abaddon," she said.

"Hmm! Who is Abaddon?" the chief wrinkled up his forehead as he inquired.

Staring at Chief Mitchell as if he were ignorant for not knowing, she answered as such, "You probably only know him as Satan."

At that moment, the chief wasn't sure if Staci really was crazy or was just acting like it to get away with murder. Not wanting to hear any more about the devil, he steered the conversation in another direction.

"Can you show us exactly where you buried the bodies?"

"Oh, yes, I have been living in close proximity to them for the past three years."

"Where have you been living?"

"In an abandoned cabin near Crater Lake. It once belonged to my parents."

A new wave of shivers ran up and down the chief's spine as his eyes widened. He was disappointed in himself, knowing that his crew went there and found nothing. Maybe, he should have gone along with them. Maybe, they should have spent more time searching in that location. He was given the information and didn't take it seriously enough.

"You mean to tell me; you've been living in the same house your parents were killed in?"

"Yes, it's still my home," she answered as if he were stupid for asking.

"How have you survived there for three years?"

"Oh, I prepared way in advance. I stored up food and supplies for two years in preparation. Plus, I have a green thumb and have a beautiful garden there."

"Okay, I think I've heard enough for now. I'm going to step out and call a team of investigators who'll go with us to the burial site."

"That's fine," she answered as if giving the chief permission.

"You are willing to lead us to the site?" he asked as he rose from his chair.

"Yes, certainly I will," she pleasantly answered.

As he stepped out, he motioned to Jackson to keep both eyes on her. He purposely left the recorder on, just in case.

He stepped into the interrogation room and called his good friend of over thirty years, Jose Gonzales, head of the FBI's Homicide division in Oregon. They had worked many cases together, including the Webber case, and they kept in touch concerning several other unsolved crimes. Their wives were good friends, as well. The two couples had spent many afternoons over dinner with the two men discussing investigations, and the two women planning their next vacation together. When they were all younger, in their mid-twenties, their favorite trip was spent diving and fishing in Belize. Twenty-five years later, they still reminisced about it almost every time they visited, promising each other to go back.

"Jose, I hope you have a minute to talk. You're not going to believe this."

Laughing, he answered, "John, even if I didn't, I always have time for you, my friend."

"I have a bombshell to drop on you. It was just dropped on me."

Jose was always laughing and smiling. That is why the chief loved him so much.

In his good-humored way, he responded, "If you can take it, I know it won't be a problem for a big guy like me." Jose was only 5' 4".

Laughing heartily, the chief replied, "Your wife tells me otherwise."

"My wife won't even talk to dirty old men like you, unless I'm around to protect her," Jose laughed.

"When is the last time you had to work late?" asked Mitchell.

"Last Thursday, why?"

"No wonder, that's when your wife had dinner with me, and she had plenty to say," he chided.

Unscathed, Jose responded, "I'm gonna have to spank her when I get home."

"Now, now, enough of that. I don't want to cause any home violence, so I'll just tell you why I called. As I said, you're not going to believe this. A woman walked into the precinct today and turned herself in."

"You're right; I don't believe it. A woman walked into your precinct," he teased.

"It gets even better," the chief said, ignoring the wisecrack.

"Well, don't keep me in suspense. Tell me who it was."

"I'm gonna name the crime, and you're gonna name the slime."

"Oh, goody, I love games," Jose answered laughing.

"She just turned herself in for murdering and burying her family here in Klamath."

Jose's smiling lips disappeared immediately, and he stood up in shock. There was only one missing family in that location, and he remembered the scene well. Ryan's words had haunted him for the last three years.

"No, don't tell me it was Mrs. Webber."

"You guessed it."

"Man, I knew it all along. That little kid across the street—what was his name?"

"Ryan."

"Yeah, Ryan. He had me convinced, even though he's just a kid. She's there now?"

"Sitting at my desk. She came in here asking for me by name, which really creeps me out. She's a strange one."

"Wow, that gives me intense goosebumps, man. So, let me get this straight, she walked right in and admitted that she killed all of them?"

"She did."

"Did she tell you what she did with the bodies?"

"She said she buried them near Crater Lake. And get this, her parents had a lake house near Crater Lake where they were murdered when she was only eleven. Apparently, she was in her bedroom asleep and never heard gunfire. She was under suspicion by the locals, but they couldn't pin it on her. And get this! For the past three years, she's been living in that same house that her parents were murdered in."

"What the hell? You have got to be kidding me. Didn't her husband know what he was marrying?"

"I doubt it."

"Okay, brother, let's make this happen. I'll make some phone calls, and you'll have a lot of back up real soon."

"Thanks, my friend."

"I'm not going to miss this. I'll be there too. Whatever you do, don't let this get out. We don't need the news crews screwing up the investigation or better yet, beating us to the site. That's embarrassing," he chuckled.

"That's for sure," the chief agreed.

ഇൻൽ

Early the next morning, Jose arrived first. Then, the FBI, including the Homicide division and the forensic team, infiltrated the small Klamath police station.

Mrs. Webber was taken from her temporary holding cell back to the interrogation room and questioned all over again, which upset her. Because they agitated her, she confessed to murdering her family but refused to cooperate and give them any further details.

"I turned myself in. If I wouldn't have, you would have never found me. Why should I tell my story over and over again? I refuse. I'll tell the complete story only one more time, and that will be in court."

"Mrs. Webber, I thought you said you were ready to confess?" Jose kindly asked. He already realized the ball was in her court and thought niceness might prevail.

"Jose, I like you. But these other guys have already greatly disturbed me. Don't take it personally, but I'm done for now."

Jose had met many criminals like her before. He could see that she liked being in control. He knew that it was best to let her have her way, this time.

"Yes, ma'am," he manipulatively complied.

"That'll be enough gentlemen," he explained to the investigators.

He and Chief Mitchell were ready to get on the road anyway.

❧ ❦ ❧

As the caravan drove toward Crater Lake, Mrs. Webber uncomfortably sat in the backseat of John and Jose's vehicle with the handcuffs cutting into her wrist.

"I turned myself in, so why do I need to wear these?" she kindly argued. "I have no intention of going anywhere but to prison, and if you don't take these off, I'm not going to show you where they're buried," she boldly stated. They looked at each other, wondering what the other thought about taking the cuffs off. Jose tilted his head and gave his "whatever" half-turned-up lip gesture to John and asked, "She doesn't have any weapons on her, right?"

"No. She's been processed."

"Well, I'm okay with taking them off, if you are," said Jose.

John bobbed his head toward Staci, gesturing for Jose to take the cuffs off and stated, "When we get there, they're back on."

"Thank you, Jose," she said in a rather seductive tone.

They knew her type and couldn't be fooled any longer. Not now, but when they were younger, it was a different story. The women they had dealt with for so many years were basically all the same. They all thought they could easily deceive men with seduction. If that didn't work, they would try crying.

They just looked at each other and rolled their eyes. It no longer flattering them.

Through all of their years of working together, they learned to play good cop/bad cop very well. They would wait and watch for the criminal's reaction to each of them before deciding who would play which role. The bad guys always seemed to like one of them, but not the other. Usually, they liked Jose better and didn't seem to care too much for John. The two couples had discussed the topic over dinner several times and couldn't come up with a clear reason as to why. John had always teased Jose saying, "It takes one to know one. They like you because you're one of them."

John pulled over to the shoulder and stopped the vehicle so Jose could get out of the car and take Mrs. Webber's handcuffs off. Since they were in the lead, the entire caravan followed the lead and pulled off onto the shoulder. As Jose was taking care of the handcuffs, John radioed to his followers that all was well, but didn't give any details as to why they had stopped. He was too embarrassed to admit that they had stopped the entire caravan to appease the criminal in the back seat.

"Ma'am, can you tell us where we're headed?" politely asked Jose. He had also learned to turn the tables and take advantage of women that were trying to flatter him.

"Crater Lake National Park," she answered.

"That's a very big park isn't it?" Jose asked.

"Very," she responded.

"Well, can you narrow it down for me?" he asked with a smile.

"Not far from *The Lady in the Woods*."

With a puzzled look, Jose asked, "What lady?"

"Oh, you've never heard of the famous sculpture?"

"No, please fill me in," he answered shaking his head.

"I'm fascinated by her because she represents so many things true in my life."

She continued as they drove toward the site as if she were the tour guide for the park.

"Dr. Earl Russell Bush was the creator of *The Lady in the Woods*. He was stationed there in 1917 and attended to the road crew that built the first rim around the lake. He had spare time on his hands and so decided to attempt, for his very first time, sculpting a figure into the side of this great boulder that was lodged among the trees. He sculpted a lady, an incomplete lady, relaxed against a volcanic rock as though she were a sleeping beauty awaiting the day her master would arrive to complete her."

They listened to her as investigators listen, with an open ear to gain insight into her character. Wanting her to feel completely comfortable and unthreatened, they let her continue without interruption.

"At Crater Lake, winter can last more than seven months. One sign of the upcoming spring is when enough snow melts to reveal *The Lady of the Woods*. The Lady and her surroundings remind me so much of myself and my life. I have also been asleep, waiting for so long for my master to complete me," she said slowly, expressing her endurance.

John and Jose eyed each other without being conspicuous and let her continue on.

"That's where you'll find my family. The snow hasn't started to fall yet, but will soon cover everything in sight—*The Lady in the Woods* and my family's burial site included. It's a beautiful place, and I wish that their bodies didn't have to be disturbed. But I know they will."

Neither John nor Jose dared to ask Mrs. Webber any questions or comment on her story of *The Lady in the Woods*. They were both sensing that Mrs. Webber was mentally unstable. Both career officers knew from experience that the unstable often misconstrue commentary. When the two were younger and inexperienced, they had made those mistakes. So now, they weren't going to take a chance of that happening. Listening was their motive.

After an hour and forty-five minutes, they drove through the park entrance. The wooden entrance sign was swinging from what looked like a tree trunk sticking out of the side of a massive rocked column. It read "North Entrance."

"How big is this park?" asked the chief.

"Two hundred and eighty-six square miles," answered Mrs. Webber.

"If it's a national park, how is it that your family had a house here? I didn't think that was allowed."

"The house is right outside the perimeter of the park. It's the only one of its kind. There are no others around. It was built out of the stones from this area before the park was officially opened in 1902. No one knows exactly when or who built it, but it was a marvel for its time. It was passed down from my grandfather to my father. And, apparently, it was passed on to my grandfather when his father died in prison. Of course, it's no longer in good condition."

Taken aback by her statement, Jose and John eyed each other, wondering which one would ask the obvious question.

But Staci, not considering her story to be relevant, directed them to drive further into the park, toward the visitor's center.

Since Jose was playing the "good cop," he spoke up.

"Just out of curiosity, what was your great-grandfather in prison for?"

Her facial expression revealed that she had started a conversation meant to be left undisturbed. But then she shrugged her shoulders, sighed deeply, and began her story.

"I guess at this point, keeping family secrets no longer matters. So I'll go ahead and tell you. My great-grandfather was convicted of murdering his parents. Story is, his attorney saved his life with the insanity plea. They diagnosed him with schizophrenia after he told them about the voices instructing him to kill his parents," she rambled on. "But I know the real truth. He wasn't schizophrenic. He was a Nephilim, like me. I know you probably won't believe me, but our ancestors were fallen angels."

John and Jose's eyes grew to the size of saucers as they listened.

"How old was your great-grandfather, if you don't mind me asking?" inquired Jose completely ignoring her spooky comment on fallen angels. Jose was religious, and he was afraid of evil spirits. So much so, that he didn't believe in speaking about them. He didn't want to give evil an invitation.

"He was eighteen—just old enough to be tried as an adult," she answered.

"Had he already had your grandfather?" asked Jose.

"No. That leads to yet another family secret," she chuckled. "My grandfather was actually born in prison. When he was born, his mother wanted nothing to do with him and signed him over to social services. He was adopted right away." She paused as if she would end her story there. John and Jose breathlessly waited hoping she would continue.

"I have told no one this story. No one has ever known about this. Only my grandparents and parents knew of it. But now it no longer matters since I'm the last one remaining in my family. Of course, there are plenty other fallen angels to carry on until the end. So, I'll tell you everything. It is very interesting anyway. Where was I?" she asked.

"Your grandfather was adopted right away," answered Jose.

"Oh, yes. Then, my grandfather had a fine upbringing with his adopted parents. He grew up and got married to my grandmother. And, like so many other adopted people, he wondered about his biological parents. I'm not sure how, but somehow he obtained their names and found them. He read all the information he could get his hands on. And even after learning what they had done, he still wanted to meet them. So he made a trip to the prison where he was allowed to meet his father, who by that time, had grown old. His mother, on the other hand, had already died. Grandfather was met with open arms by his old father. During their meeting, while the guards were not looking, my great grandfather slipped my grandfather a letter and grandfather quickly slipped it into his pocket. No one knew about the letter. I don't think even my father knew about it. I don't think that my grandfather even told my grandmother about it. My best guess is he was afraid of the power that the letter possessed."

At that point, John almost laughed out loud as he watched Jose squirming in his seat. John knew how superstitious Jose was.

"By the time I was born, both of my grandparents had passed away in a tragic car accident. But before he died, my grandfather had placed my great grandfather's letter in a sealed mason jar and hid it in the attic of our lake house. The whole time I was growing up, something, something very powerful drew me to the attic. I spent hours and hours looking in every nook and cranny. I just knew there was something up there that I was destined to find. I looked each summer that we spent there and finally found it when I was eleven. From another realm, my great-grandfather led me to his letter. I finally found it on the highest shelf on the back wall of the attic. I stood on an old dusty chair to reach it. The jar was so dusty; I couldn't see through it. I unscrewed the lid, and there it was. It was still in mint condition and easy to read. After I read it, I burned it. It was only for me to see. The moment I finished reading the letter of my great grandfather's ancestry of the fallen angels, I too was able to hear the voices. They instructed me to begin my mission by ending my parent's lives. So, that very night, I did. They never found proof or convicted me of murdering them. But I am now confessing that I am the one that shot them while they slept. Being convicted at that time wasn't part of the great plan. Now, it no longer matters. And, don't be surprised if I decide not to tell anyone else about my heritage. We don't want too many people to know. We'd rather have the upper hand. Oh, and if you find my story absurd, there is proof. You can read Genesis Chapter 6. It tells of the sons of God being with the daughters of men. It can also be found in the book of Enoch and The Dead Sea Scrolls. I read everything I could get my hands on when I first found out. It's fascinating," she ended with a proud smile.

Over their long career dealing with criminals, John and Jose thought they had heard it all. But they had never heard anything quite like that before. They weren't sure what to do, for it had, all of a sudden, become quite overwhelming. Individually, they both decided to take care of the current problem first.

As they drove up to the visitor's center, Mrs. Webber pointed and said, "Stop over there at the far left side of the parking area."

The visitor's center was made out of stones, as the chief imagined the house was. It was off-season, and there were no visitors, which everyone was glad for. They wanted no publicity.

"I hope you guys are in good shape because it's about an hour and a half hike through the hemlocks. There used to be a road going straight to the house, but after my parents' death, they closed it. Now, trees and shrubbery have covered it over, so there's no road, only a small pathway."

Both of their faces turned downward. Neither were young men any longer. Nor, were they in good shape.

"Great," said Chief John Mitchell in a displeased tone.

"How did you get all three bodies up there?" curiously asked Jose.

"One at a time," answered Mrs. Webber with a half-smile, which disgusted the two officers and put an end to any more questions.

"Your handcuffs will have to be put back on, Ma'am," said Jose.

"I understand," she said, staring him in the eye and holding her hands out toward him. Trying not to have any skin-to-skin contact with her, Jose, feeling cold all over, placed the cuffs back on her.

The forensic team was busy unloading all of their equipment when Chief Mitchell walked to their vehicle.

"Travel light as possible. She tells us that there is no road, and it's an hour's hike through the woods."

"What? That bitch could have told us that before we drove all the way out here. I could have brought a wagon," stated Elijah, head of their forensics unit.

"I don't guess there's a Walmart around," said his assistant, trying to lighten the tension.

Elijah, shaking his head and looking at all their equipment in the back of the van said, "Everyone will have to help. I need all of this equipment."

He had stressed *everyone,* and John and Jose knew what he meant. He wanted to make Mrs. Webber help carry equipment to punish her for not letting them know in advance.

44

The chief shaking his head, immediately spoke up, "You know we can't take the cuffs off."

Rearing up, Elijah asked, "Why not? I'm not scared of her, are you?"

Elijah had never been a blessing to work with. It was as though he had to prove that he wasn't a saint, as his name implied. Plus, everyone knew that the only reason Elijah was able to reach the position he held was because his father was the County Sheriff.

He was young and untrained in getting along with others. Everyone knew it but had to put up with him because of who he was.

Resisting the instinct to slam Elijah to the ground and plant a fist into his face, Chief Mitchell forced himself to calmly and flatly state, "Elijah, you are not running this show. This is not your call. The handcuffs are not coming off, and everyone but her will help carry equipment."

"Fine," Elijah snapped as he started forcefully pulling equipment out and dropping it to the ground without any regard for its integrity.

Everyone stayed back as he let his temper fly. Before he had finished, everyone could see him quickly running out of energy, as he wastefully spent most of it. Then they dared get close enough to start picking up the equipment. Once it was all picked up, and everyone was loaded down like pack horses, Mrs. Webber directed them to the back of the visitor's center. Barely visible was an opening in the thick shrubbery that they would not have seen if she hadn't shown them. Loaded down with shovels, picks, cameras, and all of the other forensic equipment, they began their long, single-file hike down the overgrown path.

The temperature was comfortable at about 75 degrees, and it was accompanied with a nice warm breeze. The leaves and trees were draped alike in red, orange, and yellow shades of fall, as the sweet, fresh air gently propelled them upward. If not for the dreaded duty ahead and the heavy equipment, it would have been a lovely hike.

About an hour down the path, they reached the carving that Staci had earlier told John and Jose about.

"There she is, waiting patiently for the right moment," delightfully acknowledged Mrs. Weber as she pointed toward the statue.

Everyone had grown quite sore and cranky from carrying their heavy loads, while twigs and branches slapped them in their faces. They were not in the least bit interested in the statue. They just wanted to reach their destination and drop the heavy equipment.

"The right moment for what? Once your stone cold, there is nothing else," spouted Elijah with a smirk.

"That's where you're wrong, young man. Death is actually where life begins," stated Mrs. Webber.

"One thing I know everything about is the afterlife," said Elijah with a patience in his demeanor that the others didn't know he had. "My parents made sure of that. I know that it says in the Bible to be absent from the body is to be present with God. But I was actually talking about your stone cold personality. Someone that kills their family is stone cold. You won't be with God once you're put to death. You're going straight to hell, lady."

"Yes, I am, and that's where my new life will begin. Did your parents also teach you the part of the Bible that says the devil roams the earth like a roaring lion, seeking whom he may devour?" Mrs. Webber asked as if she were interested in teaching Elijah.

"Of course, they did, but that has nothing to do with you."

"You're incorrect. The devil has many, many angels of his own, each with one purpose in mind—to destroy God's creation, mankind. I will be very much alive assisting my master, Abaddon, in the final destruction. You can join us if you'd like," she said with pure evil in her voice.

"You should easily be able to get off on the insanity plea. You're a wack job," he stated as he turned and walked away from her ending their conversation. He wouldn't admit it nor show it, but she made him uneasy. Each of them studied the statue as they passed by. It was just as she had described—a lady lounging on a huge stone that was lodged in some trees. One could only see the back of the naked lady. Her face and frontal view could only be imagined by each onlooker.

About an hour past the carving, just as Mrs. Webber had stated, they reached a clearing with a small stone cabin in the center of it. Most of the glass in the windows was broken. Duct tape and small pieces of scrap wood awkwardly took its place. Only a few boards remained on the front porch, and the rest had fallen to the ground below. The roof was waved like the ocean and pitted with holes as if hailstones had rained down on it. But most of the stone on the walls was still sturdy.

"This is where I have lived for the past three years, awaiting the right time to emerge," she broke the silence, as everyone was studying the surroundings.

No one said a word. It was a somber moment, as they waited for her to relinquish her family's gravesite. After what she had done, no one really cared where or how she had lived for the last three years. They stood motionless, still loaded down with all of the heavy equipment.

"They are buried around back," she said, as she finally realized they were waiting for her direction.

In unison, they followed her lead to the back of the stone cabin. The backyard had been cleared, and there was a flourishing vegetable garden with, what looked like to the chief, broccoli, onions, potatoes, carrots, and turnips. As she walked past her garden, she looked at the chief and bragged, "You asked how I survived. I'm quite good at it."

Next to the garden was a tree stump, with a hatchet buried into the top of it. Next to the tree stump lay a pile of freshly cut firewood she had obviously cut for herself.

"This way," she said, as she led them away from the back of the house toward the wooded area.

"How much further?" Elijah immediately barked.

"It's right here," she answered as she stopped only about ten feet inside the uncleared woods.

The ground was covered with leaves and branches. No one could see anything resembling grave sites. Everyone's eyes were searching to and fro to no avail.

"Where?" asked the chief, as his head darted around searching for the site.

"Right there," she said pointing directly in front of them.

He squinted his eyes to focus where she was pointing. Finally, he saw three stones all in a row. They were barely visible as the tips peeked up through the leaves and other fallen debris. Elijah dropped his equipment, loudly disturbing the peacefulness of the forest. With the camera that was hanging around his neck, he began snapping pictures of the barely visible stones. Then, he knelt down and began digging for something in one of the bags. He quickly retrieved a brush, walked over to the stones, and began brushing the debris off of them.

The rest of them quietly laid their equipment down. After Elijah had brushed all the debris away from the three stones, he stepped back next to the others. In silence, they all read the names on the makeshift headstones.

In each cream-colored stone, was carved a name, a birth date, and the day of their death. All three stones shared one common trait—the death date.

The first to the left read, Sam Webber, July 12, 1972 – Sept. 7, 2011. The middle stone read Andrew Webber, Sept. 29, 2001 – Sept. 7, 2011, and the last to the right read, Elizabeth Webber. Nov. 1, 2004 – Sept. 7, 2011.

Several in the group dropped their heads in sorrow, while others looked at Mrs. Webber, wondering how she could have done this to her own family. She stood with no sign of guilt or sorrow. She seemed only to wonder when they would begin digging. Elijah walked over to Chief Mitchell, put his hand on his shoulder, and humbly said, "I'm sorry for my behavior. You were right."

Chief Mitchell patted Elijah on the back and said, "It's okay, son. Let's get to work."

They started with Sam Webber's grave, first removing his stone and then carefully removing the chunks of dirt that lay over his remains. As Staci had warned, the grave was shallow. She had buried her family only one foot into the ground. Only their skeletons remained and none of the tissue after three years in the shallow graves. As the team unearthed each one, Staci gave details as to why she chose the clothing they were buried in. No one really wanted to hear what she had to say, but curiosity kept them listening.

"Sam always joked about being buried in his favorite clothes, his San Francisco 49ers jersey and his favorite blue jeans," she said while lovingly smiling down at his remains dressed in exactly that.

"I placed a picture of his mother and father between his hands. He talked about them all the time. He loved them more than he loved me," she concluded as she turned away from her husband's gravesite and toward the cabin. As she looked away, several of the detectives glanced at each other in bewilderment over her remarks.

Apparent to everyone was the manner in which Sam Webber had died. His skull had obviously been crushed.

Once the forensic team completed gathering Sam's remains, they removed the headstone of the middle grave, Andrew's. This one was especially tough for Chief Jack Mitchell, as he recalled several personal conversations with Andrew and his friend Ryan. They removed the larger chunks of dirt and brushed off the lighter. And, once again, the team had to hear another nightmarish narrative from Mrs. Webber.

"When I first bought that Oregon Duck's t-shirt for him, he wore it three days in a row. And, I swear, he never took that baseball cap off."

Even though the Oregon Ducks baseball cap was covering the top portion of the boy's skull, crushed areas peeked from beneath the brim.

The third grave marked *Elizabeth* was much smaller. Again, they carefully excavated the site to find the same pose constricted on Elizabeth—tiny skeletal arms crossed with tiny hand bones laying flat over the ribs. The most crushing results were exhibited on her skull. Parts of the skull were broken off and had fallen within.

"How old was she, Ma'am?" asked Elijah.

"Seven," answered Mrs. Webber.

"My daughter is seven," he said, as he sternly gazed at Mrs. Webber.

"I loved them very much. You wouldn't understand," she sneered at him.

"You're right. I don't," he sneered back.

All of the skeletal remains were bagged and tagged. Usually, the forensic team would find other evidence at a makeshift burial, but not these. Mrs. Webber had everything nice and tidy, as she did everything else in her life.

Chapter 5
The Confession

Mrs. Webber was assigned an attorney—a very young and inexperienced defense attorney by the name of Harold Green. Knowing that Staci Webber had already admitted guilt, Mr. Green felt that he had been given a shoddy first case. But at the same time, he was grateful for any experience. Little did he know how big his name would become for representing Mrs. Webber.

Harold asked that Mrs. Webber be placed in the interrogation room for their initial meeting. Mrs. Webber could hear the uneasiness in the young man's voice as he introduced himself and nervously shook hands with her. One of Mrs. Webber's pet peeves was when a man extended his hand out for her to shake.

"Mrs. Webber, I am Harold Green. I have been assigned to your case," he stated as he extended his hand.

"Mr. Green, how old are you?" she asked.

Belittled at her question, he answered, "Ma'am, I'm old enough to have an attorney's license and be assigned to represent you."

"But you're obviously not old enough to have learned some manners," she attacked.

"I'm sorry. I don't know what you're talking about?" he answered while pulling his hand back as if afraid she would bite it.

"Apparently no one has taught you that it is rude to extend your hand to a woman. We know what you do with that hand. You probably just went to the bathroom to relieve yourself and didn't bother to wash your hands. And, if I would have shaken your hand, I would have your privates on my hand. You are supposed to wait for the women to extend her hand first. If she doesn't, then you simply don't shake hands," she scolded.

Embarrassed, Harold Green meekly responded, "Sorry ma'am!"

"Now let's start over, shall we?" she strongly suggested.

Nodding his head in agreement, he said in a meek voice and his hands in his pocket, "I'm Harold Green and have been assigned to represent you."

Smiling, Mrs. Webber said, "Much better. Now let's get down to business."

"Okay, the first thing I would like to discuss with you is the plea bargain. I realize you have already admitted guilt, but we can still use the insanity defense."

"Sorry, young man, but I refuse to do that."

"But, ma'am, capital punishment is legal in the state of Oregon."

"Yes, I realize that."

"Your crime is considered aggravated murder and in Oregon is the only crime subject to the penalty of death. You will receive either death, imprisonment without parole, or life imprisonment."

"I choose death," she said without remorse.

"But, Mrs. Webber, I think you have a very good chance if we plead insanity," he innocently informed her.

"Young man, we need to get something straight right here and now. I am in charge of my life, not you," she softly informed. "I will tell you what we're going to do, not the reversal. I'm going to get the death penalty. That is our plan."

Confused about what his plan of action would be if it wasn't to win the case, he simply said, "Yes, ma'am."

"I want my trial to begin as soon as possible, so I can be transferred to Oregon State Penitentiary."

"May I ask why you're in such a hurry to be convicted guilty and transferred to prison?"

"It's all part of the great plan," she said with a smile.

Harold Green was feeling very frustrated and wanted to appeal the court's decision for him to represent Mrs. Webber, but knew that was not possible. He felt that his whole career was in jeopardy.

"Okay, ma'am. Since I have been assigned to represent you, I need to know all the facts before we head into court."

"There really isn't a lot of information I wish to share. The only information anyone needs to know is this: I selected a stone for each of my family members. I engraved each of their names, birth dates, and death dates into the stones. Then, I took those stones and crushed their skulls while they slept so they wouldn't feel a thing. Then, I buried them using those same stones as their headstones. I waited until the time was right to confess, and here we are."

Stunned, he answered, "Yes ma'am, here we are. That should do it for me, but the judge may want more details, such as why you murdered them."

"Since you're my attorney, I'll tell you the truth. But no one else needs to know because no one would believe it anyway. You see, I have to go away. They couldn't be left without a mother."

"Where do you have to go?"

"This will be the last time that I'll tell anyone. So, listen carefully. I am going to Sheol to assist Abaddon in the great destruction."

"Who is Abaddon?" he asked with a scowl on his face.

"You may not know him by that name. Do you know the Bible at all?"

"Yes, ma'am."

"Then you probably know him as Lucifer or Satan."

"Oh," he said with wide eyes.

"I see doubt in your eyes. I thought you said you knew the Bible?"

"I do."

"Then why are you doubting?"

"I don't know ma'am. I think that will do it for today," he said helplessly.

"That's fine. But don't ask me again. This matter is closed. Please have my trial set as soon as possible!"

"You can bet I will. Honestly, ma'am, I want to get this over as fast as you do."

Smiling, she nodded, "Thank you!"

"Thank you, ma'am!" he said on the way out. The guard stepped in and took Mrs. Webber back to her cell, where she would stay for the next two months.

"Lord, help me!" Harold Green whispered as he walked down the hall. "What did I do to deserve this?"

࿇

As Harold Green promised, he set the trial date as soon as possible, for December 1, 2014. He went to see her one last time before the appointed court date.

"Hello, Mrs. Webber," he said making sure not to extend his hand.

"Good day, Mr. Green. I see that my lesson was effective."

"Yes, ma'am!"

"Why has it taken so long? I thought you were going to set a court date ASAP."

"Your court date is set for December first."

"I don't understand why it took so long. I'm going to plead guilty. It's not like we are going to have a full-blown trial."

"Unfortunately, we are."

"Why?"

"Because in our justice system, your confession is treated like any other piece of evidence. A full confession does not prevent a full trial from occurring. You must still testify under oath to facts establishing your guilt."

"I see."

"The reason I'm here today is to ask you if there is anything else you need to tell me before we go to trial."

"No, nothing has changed."

"Very well then. I'll see you in two weeks."

ℰᏻℭᏰ

Two weeks came and went. The day of the trial finally arrived, and the courtroom was silent as Mrs. Webber was escorted in, shackled at the wrist and ankles. Sam's parents were seated in front alongside the prosecuting attorney. They had not seen Staci since their last visit five years earlier and, to them, she looked exactly the same. It appeared that she hadn't aged as they had over the grief of losing their beloved son and two grandchildren. Mrs. Webber was escorted to the front and sat next to her defense attorney, Harold Green.

The silence was broken when the bailiff loudly spoke, "All rise! Judge Clifton now presiding." After the judge took his seat at the front of the courtroom, the bailiff loudly announced, "Please be seated!"

"Good morning, ladies and gentlemen. Calling the case of the State of Oregon verses Staci Webber. Are both sides ready?" asked the judge.

"Yes, your honor," both sides answered.

"Will the clerk please stand and swear in the jury," asked the judge.

"Will the jury please stand and raise your right hand? Do each of you swear that you will fairly try the case before the court and return a true verdict according to evidence of the court, so help you, God? Please say I do," stated the clerk.

The jury stood, with their right hands raised, and answered, "I do."

"Please be seated," requested the clerk.

Judge Clifton continued, "The prosecuting attorney may make his opening statement."

Brent Downing, prosecuting attorney for the state of Oregon arose, pointed at Mrs. Webber, looked back and forth between the courtroom and the jury, and stated, "This is an open and shut case. This woman has already admitted guilt, but we must present the evidence to you so that there is no doubt that she, is indeed, the killer of her entire family. You will see and hear hideous facts surrounding the murders of three innocent people. While this lady looks prim and proper, please keep in mind that she is not, and consider all of the facts that you see and hear."

"The defense attorney, Harold Green, may make his opening statement," spoke the judge.

"Ladies and gentlemen of the jury, it is true that this lady has pleaded guilty, but remember our law firmly states that we are only to consider her confession of guilt as partial evidence. We must also listen to all of the other evidence. We are not to convict until all of the evidence has been presented. Please keep that in mind," spoke Harold Green.

"The prosecutor may call his first witness," spoke the judge.

"I call Chief Jack Mitchell to the stand," stated Brent Downing.

He arose, made his way to the front, and was sworn in by the clerk. After Mr. Downing had the chief introduce himself, he asked the chief to tell the jury about the investigation at the Webber's household.

"I was the first on the scene, well, besides Ryan, who was Andrew Webber's best friend and neighbor, who lives across the street. He hadn't heard from his friend in a few days and went to check on him. That's when he came upon the bloody scene. He then ran home, told his mother what he had seen, and had her call our police station. When we arrived, I walked toward the bedrooms first. That's where Ryan informed us of a massive amount of blood on the carpets. We did find blood in the carpet, the beds, and elsewhere. We secured the area, taped it off, and called forensics, the FBI, and the search team."

"Did forensics have any suggestions as to what may have happened?"

"Yes, they said that it appeared that each of the three family members had been massacred in the same fashion. It appeared that each was in bed where they suffered fatal head injuries. Copious amounts of blood were found on their pillows, and trails of blood were found leading to the garage from each bedroom. Forensics suggested that the killer crushed the heads of the victims with an unknown object while they slept. Then, the victims were dragged, one by one, to the garage where they were placed in a vehicle. That's where the trails of blood ended," completed the chief.

The prosecution called their witnesses one by one until all had their say. They included neighbors, store clerks, and friends of the Webbers—anyone that could testify on the family's lifestyle and the personality of Staci Webber.

Finally, Staci Webber herself was called to the stand, sworn in, and asked to state her name.

"Mrs. Webber, did you murder your family?" asked Brent Downing.

"I gracefully put them to rest."

"Would you like to tell the jury why?"

"Sure. I must leave, and I couldn't just leave them unattended," she said nonchalantly.

"Where must you go?"

"I refuse to discuss that at this present moment."

"Then, can you tell the jury how you put your family to rest?"

"Yes, I can. First, I retrieved three stones from Crater Lake. You can't find prettier stones anywhere. They're a beautiful cream color. I purchased an engraving tool and practiced quite a bit before I finally engraved their names into the stones. I engraved their names, birthdates, and rebirth dates."

"Rebirth dates, is that the same as death dates to you?" asked Mr. Downing.

"All of the unknowing refer to rebirth date as death date, instead."

"The unknowing? Can you clarify the meaning of the unknowing, please?"

"It's quite simple. The unknowing are all the millions of people wandering about the earth without an inkling of a clue about this present life, let alone the afterlife. They just bustle about without a care, thinking that they are doing the right thing by gathering as many material objects as they can, drinking and laughing, having a grand ol' time. They don't know the grave danger their souls are in. They don't know that they are being hunted. They don't know that they are constantly making themselves easy prey."

Realizing that Mrs. Webber could easily qualify for a mental evaluation because of her testimony, Mr. Downing was sorry that he asked for clarification and quickly ended the discussion.

"Thank you for the clarification. Please go back to where we left off. You engraved their information on the stones and then what?"

"I waited for the chosen date and started with Sam first. I knew that if he awoke while I was taking care of the children, he would try to stop me. I waited until 2:00 AM when I knew they would all be in deep sleep. I quietly made my way to the garage and took the stones out of my trunk. I took Sam's into our bedroom, climbed into bed next to him and watched him sleep for a while. I softly kissed his forehead then raised the stone above his head and brought it down on him. He never woke up. His body quivered for a few seconds, but that was it. I didn't want to wake the children, so I left him there while I finished with them. I went back to the garage and got Andrew's stone. He was a deep sleeper, so I knew he wouldn't wake up. I went into his room and watched him for a while as his eyes moved with his dreams. Then, I raised the stone above his head and brought it down. It surprised me how much easier his skull was to crush than my husbands. His nerves also caused his body to quiver. Only he quivered more strongly. I guess because he was young and strong. Then I went back to the garage and got the last stone for my baby girl, Elizabeth. I was afraid she would wake up. Since the day she was born, she was a very light sleeper. So, quietly, I crept into her room and stood next to her bed. As I raised the stone, her eyes slowly started to open, so I quickly had to bring the stone down. I didn't mean for it to crush her skull so badly. I did it too quickly," she answered with shame, as everyone in the courtroom listened in horror.

That was the only time she showed any shame or remorse. She was not ashamed of killing her entire family, but only that she crushed her daughter's head a little worse than she meant to. Brent Downing was taken by her remarks, as everyone else in the courtroom was, and knew, if desired, she was eligible for the insanity plea. Not a sound was made as Mrs. Webber spoke.

"I understand you refuse the insanity plea?" stated Brent Downing.

"Objection," stated Harold Green wondering why he should even bother.

"Sustained. Right now we are trying Mrs. Webber to decide her guilt, not her ability to stand trial," agreed the judge.

The trial continued for one week. The punishment phase, however, only took one day. Mrs. Webber received the death penalty she so desired. As in her trial proceedings, she showed no remorse nor fear.

Because of overcrowding in the Oregon state prison system, she was transferred to Texas State Penitentiary at Huntsville to the Mountain View Unit for women on death row.

While there, to everyone's confusion, she began taking

microbiology classes. No one understood why, and she refused to confide in anyone. She studied and read constantly, only taking time to sleep and eat. Everyone talked about her, even the other inmates, whom she would not socialize with. They didn't mind. No one wanted to socialize with her anyway. She was the big mystery for the next three years.

Chapter 6
Daughter-in-law Material

In another part of Texas, Mary Jane Scarsdale awoke to an uncomfortable thought. "Today, I turn 35," she unhappily muttered to herself. She was still working in the same restaurant, The Golden Skillet, that she had been working in since she was twenty-one years old. It was considered, by most of the locals, the best restaurant in her hometown of Alvin, Texas. She had worked her way up to manager, and she made enough money to pay the rent and utilities for her efficiency apartment. She could afford everything she needed, but not a lot that she wanted. She had a washer and dryer, plenty of clothes and shoes, and could afford to eat anywhere in Alvin. Of course, there were no swanky restaurants in Alvin. Mary Jane was satisfied with her Toyota Corolla, but what she really wanted to drive was a Cadillac.

Something about the age of 35 made Mary Jane very dissatisfied with her progression in life as no other age had. She couldn't help but think that by the age of 35, she should be happily married to her soul mate, have two children running and playing on their beautiful green lawn, and live in a brick house with a sparkling blue pool in the backyard. Since high school, she had her life all planned out, and so far, it had not gone according to plan.

"Exactly, where did I go wrong?" she pondered out loud.

As she lay in bed, her thoughts raced back to the innocent age of high school.

On the first day of her freshman year, Mary Jane recalled nervously looking for room 136. The bell was just about to ring, and she was going to be late for her English class. All of a sudden, she heard someone say, "What room are you looking for?"

She quickly answered, "Room 136."

"That's where I'm going. You can follow me," he said as he jetted down the hall. He was hard to keep up with, but Mary Jane managed. She sat down directly behind her knight in shining armor. During roll call, she learned that his name was Jake McCowsky.

As their freshman year progressed, so did her crush on him. He was the quarterback for the football team. He had wavy, jet black hair and muscular arms. With his looks, she thought, they would make beautiful children together. As he sat directly in front of Mary Jane during English class, she could smell his cologne. How she loved his scent. Each day during class, she would stare at the back of his head and fantasize about him holding her in his muscular arms, kissing her on the lips, and rubbing the inside of her thighs in their backyard pool—after they were married, of course.

But each day, when the bell rang, ending English class, he jumped up and sprinted down the hall toward the gym—never once noticing her. Mary Jane's young heart would break each and every time. Nevertheless, she relentlessly continued to hope, because she just knew that he was her soul mate and that they were meant to be together. She told herself time and time again that she must be patient and wait for him. Every time he passed her in the hall with the other football players, she would smile at him, but he never looked at her to notice. In passing, she must have smiled at him a hundred times or more. She kept thinking that he would eventually look her way and notice how cute she was, but he never did.

Then, to her dismay, Jake started dating a cheerleader named Cindy Lou, who was known as the prettiest girl in school. They became stuck together like glue. She hardly ever saw one without the other, and they were always arm-in-arm. They dated all throughout high school.

Of course, with their level of popularity, they were voted Prom king and queen. Mary Jane could never forget how beautiful they danced together that night. Beneath the twinkling lights, they magically danced in each other's arms. Their dance ended with Cindy Lou being delicately dipped and kissed by Jake. The crowd burst into loud cheering and applause. They curtsied and bowed to show their appreciation. Then, as the dance floor filled with everyone else, they disappeared into the crowd.

Mary Jane continued to hope that Jake would notice her, all the way up until the day he and Cindy Lou married right after graduation. It was a big event in Alvin. Everyone knew each other there, and almost everyone attended their wedding. As Mary Jane watched Cindy Lou walk down the aisle toward Jake, she just wanted to cry. After all, that was supposed to be her walking down the aisle toward Jake.

Cindy Lou and Jake were both beautiful people, perfectly fit, perfectly straight white teeth, and both came from wealthy families. Even Mary Jane had to admit, they were a gorgeous couple, and it was a beautiful wedding. During the reception, everyone ranted and raved about what a wonderful life the "perfect couple" would have together. How many children would they have? What side of town will they live on? Would Jake's dad let him start at the top of their family business or make him work his way up? Was Cindy Lou going to work or start their family right away?

"Yuck, I'm going to puke if I hear one more thing about Cindy Lou," said Mary Jane as she was driving away before the reception was over. She just couldn't fake pretending to be happy for them any longer.

Eventually, talk of the popular couple died down. After a couple of years, Cindy Lou blossomed after having two beautiful children, and Mary Jane giggled every time she saw Cindy Lou's big rear end at the grocery store. Cindy Lou and Jake both put on the pounds. They stayed married for nine years and then got a divorce. By that time, Jake was no longer attractive to Mary Jane. However, Mary Jane was still in great shape, because she worked out religiously and carefully watched what she ate.

As Mary Jane continued laying in bed reminiscing, she grinned as she remembered the day she turned the tables on Jake McCowsky.

She was working her usual shift at the restaurant when Jake, after his divorce, walked in and sat down at one of her tables. At first, Mary Jane didn't treat him any different than she treated her other customers.

"Good morning, what would you like to drink, sir?" she pleasantly asked with a friendly smile.

"Coffee, please. Didn't we go to high school together?" he asked.

Smiling, she answered, "I don't remember, did we?"

The look on his face was priceless to Mary Jane. It was obvious that he couldn't believe that someone could forget him. She felt that she had just deservingly dashed his ego to pieces.

"I'm Jake McCowsky. I was quarterback all the way through high school. Everybody knows who I am," he said in disbelief.

"Oh, well that explains it. I've never cared much for football. I'm so sorry, but I really don't remember you."

"Well, I remember you. You were that cute girl that always smiled at me in the hall," he said with a flirty smile.

"I've always been very friendly. I'll be right back with your coffee, sir?"

"Thank you," he answered with obvious confusion that any girl would blow him off. As she walked away, she thought what a jerk he was for ignoring her in high school, knowing the whole time that she was always smiling at him.

She returned with his coffee, and after he placed his order, he had that look—like he might ask her out and did try.

He asked, "Would you..." and before he could get the rest of the question out, Mary Jane began walking away, smiling ear to ear. "I'll be right back with your order, sir," she purposely interrupted.

He didn't try to make any more small talk with Mary Jane. He just quietly sat and ate his food by himself. After that incident, Mary Jane saw Jake in town a few times throughout the years, but he never approached her or tried to hit on her again.

"Funny how things work out," thought Mary Jane as she decided to get out of bed and focus on the future instead of the past.

"Today is the first day of the rest of your life," Mary Jane said out loud trying to encourage herself. As she looked in the closet for something to wear, she wondered, "What will I do today to make my life what I want it to be?" Then, something her Dad always says popped into her mind. She chuckled and stated her dad's advice out loud, "If you don't like something, change it. That's just what I'm going to do. I'm tired of my life. I want a better job, and I want to meet my soul mate and marry him."

She began working on her plan that very day because Mary Jane was the kind of girl that didn't mess around once she had made up her mind.

That very morning, on her birthday, she called a job placement agency in Houston. It just so happen that there was an immediate opening that afternoon, which she eagerly accepted.

Mary Jane didn't like going to Houston. She didn't like the traffic and the large crowds. A couple of her friends had moved from Alvin to Houston in order to make better money. But every time Mary Jane went there, she was reminded how wonderful and peaceful it was in her small town. Luckily, the agency was on the edge of Houston, so she didn't have to travel too far in.

As she pulled up to the ten-story black building, her palms began to sweat. "Why am I so nervous?" she asked herself. At that moment, reality sunk in. She realized that she had stayed in one spot for so long that she had become settled in her ways, something she often heard old people talk about.

"Well, that really does it. I need to take a challenging job—one that will get me out of my comfort zone and out of my town before it's too late," she thought.

Her first impulse was to get back into her car and go home. Instead, she looked up at the tall building, took a deep breath, and started walking.

Once inside, she felt much better as the tranquility overtook her. The lobby was nicely decorated to resemble an outdoor terrace with a bountiful number of clay pots filled with trees and ivy. There was even a pianist in the center playing beautiful music, as people sat listening on comfortable couches and chairs. As she walked through the center of the attentive audience, she passed a water fountain with small goldfish peacefully swimming in circles. On the other side of the lobby were glass elevators, which took her all the way up to the tenth floor. As the elevator rose, she watched the pianist get smaller and smaller. When she stepped off the elevator, she could still hear the music from below. She peered over the balcony and could see the same crowd was still in attendance. She located the suite she was looking for, took a deep breath, and entered. The receptionist looked like she had bleached blond hair, heaps of makeup, and if she bent over to pick something up, her breasts would flop out. People didn't dress like that where Mary Jane came from. The whole town would talk about them. She tried to focus on her face and not let her eyes roam, but she couldn't help it. Mary Jane was relieved when she had finished giving the receptionist her personal information and could just sit and wait her turn.

There were two other women waiting for interviews. They were both pretty dolled up too with short skirts and low-cut blouses. She couldn't help but feel out of place with very little makeup, black slacks, and a white blouse. She wondered if they would all be interviewed by a man. Why else would the others be dressed like they were?

"They look slutty. I'm so uncomfortable," she thought as she quietly sat waiting.

Finally, it was her turn, and the receptionist called Mary Jane's name. "Follow me, please," said the receptionist.

As Mary Jane followed her, she couldn't help but stare at how short her skirt was as her fanny swayed back and forth in it. The receptionist's high heels clicked loudly on the floor as she escorted Mary Jane to the back of the large open room. She led her to the desk of a mature lady at the very back.

"Mrs. Wilson, Ms. Scarsdale," quickly spoke the receptionist as she turned and walked away.

Mary Jane watched the older lady at the desk shake her head in disgust as she watched the receptionist sachet her way back to the front. Redirecting her attention, the elderly lady said, "Hi, my name is Gertrude Wilson. Please have a seat!"

"Thank you!" said Mary Jane with her friendliest smile even though she felt caught in the crossfire of an unspoken rivalry.

"I have been looking over your application and see that you are interested in changing careers."

"Yes, ma'am. I would like something different. I've been waiting tables my whole life, and I need a big change," she explained.

"Even though you don't have a lot of experience, I see that you have a solid work history. Companies like it when they hear someone has worked at the same location for extended periods, and you have been with your employer for fifteen years," encouraged Gertrude.

"I actually hadn't thought of that as an asset," admitted Mary Jane.

"It is. As a matter of fact, I have a company that is looking for someone just like you. They want a real person, not someone that spends hours making themselves look like something they're not," she whispered, leaning toward Mary Jane as she nodded her head toward the receptionist. It was almost as though Mrs. Wilson and Mary Jane were automatic cohorts against the receptionist.

"Yeah, I can't be something I'm not. But I didn't know there were companies looking for that," Mary Jane said while feeling more confident about her appearance.

"Young lady, one of the most important things you need to learn in life is to always show confidence in yourself, even when you're not. If you're confident, people will sense that, and they too will have confidence in you. On the flip side, if you let your guard down and show weakness, they'll have absolutely no confidence in you. I like to say, 'fake it till you make it.' If I send you on an interview, can you do that? Can you show total confidence?"

"I think so."

"We're going to practice that as we interview. I want you to realize that you can do the job that I send you to or I wouldn't be sending you there. I've been doing this a long time. Do you trust me?"

"Yes, ma'am, I actually do."

"See how my confidence encourages you to trust me?"

"Yes, ma'am, I see that."

"Good! Now, let me ask you some questions and get to know you better. As you probably sense, I'm not conventional. I'm old school. I'm going to be asking you some rather personal questions to make sure that I put your personality in where it fits, so both you and your employer will be happy. Are you willing to answer some rather personal questions in order to be properly fitted?"

"Yes, ma'am. I don't mind at all."

Smiling with approval, Mrs. Wilson scribbled something on her pad.

"Very good, then. We will begin. Oh, and don't worry dear. Everything that I write down is only for me. As soon as we're done, I'll shred all of your personal information."

"Okay."

"Let's start with your name, Mary Jane Scarsdale. Are you named after anyone?"

"Yes, my grandmother," she proclaimed proudly.

As Mrs. Wilson wrote, she asked another question.

"Are you in a committed relationship?"

As Mary Jane's forehead crinkled with confusion as to why that was pertinent, she answered, "No, ma'am, I'm not."

"Have you ever been married?"

That question tensed her even more than the previous, and she answered hesitantly, "No, ma'am."

Mary Jane was beginning to think that Mrs. Wilson might be a little too old and senile to be working.

"Do you desire to be in a personal relationship?"

"Yes, ma'am, I do," she answered uncomfortably as she looked around the room to see if anyone was listening in.

"How many locations have you lived in for the past fifteen years?"

"Only two."

"Describe them please."

"My parents' house, which is just a little three-bedroom wooden house out on a country road in Alvin. I moved out of my parents' house after I graduated into an apartment not far from them."

"Great! You show extreme stability. How many boyfriends have you had?"

Mary Jane thought, *There is no way this has anything to do with a job.*

"Three," she answered anyway.

"Do you have any children?"

"No."

"Do you want any?"

"Yes, when I meet the right man and I'm married."

"Would you consider yourself an old-fashioned girl?"

"Yes."

"Do you go to church?"

"Yes, ma'am."

"Are your parents still married, and do you believe in the phrase, 'until death do us part?'"

"Yes, they are. They've been married for fifty-five years, and I hope to be able to say the same one day. I'll never divorce. I don't believe in it."

Mrs. Wilson seemed to really like that answer as she showed her approval with a big smile.

"It says here on your résumé that you have had only one job and that's at a restaurant called The Golden Skillet. Is that correct? You haven't left anything out?"

"No, ma'am, that's the only place I've worked. I started there when I was sixteen, cleaning tables. After several years, I was promoted to manager."

"Why are you looking for another job?"

"It's a good job; I just want something better for myself. The truth is, today's my thirty-fifth birthday, and I feel like I have to make a move now."

"Oh, well, happy birthday!"

"Thank you."

"Believe me, I do understand what birthdays can do to a girl," she said nodding her head. "Sometimes they make you reevaluate your whole life, and they give you an uncomfortable sense of urgency to change it."

"That is exactly what this birthday's done!"

"Well, I think I can help you. I really think I have the perfect place for you," smiled Mrs. Wilson.

"But I do have a few more questions to ask. Would you consider yourself patient with people in general?"

With a renewed sense of hope, Mary Jane answered, "Yes, ma'am."

"Since you are from a small town, you have only been around people that you know, correct?"

"Well, no, not exactly. Strangers do come through all the time to eat at our restaurant since it's right on the main highway."

"Do you ever get obnoxious customers?"

"Oh, yes. Of course," Mary Jane answered.

"And, how do you handle them?"

"I'm polite to them, but I'm happy when they leave."

"Excellent! Because the position I have in mind for you requires the ability to handle unruly personalities. But working directly at your side would be excellent people such as yourself. However, I do have one concern. If you do decide to take this position, you'll have to stretch yourself a bit. Being from a small town, I don't believe you've ever been to a place quite like this before."

"Where is it?" Mary Jane asked with intense curiosity.

"Before I tell you where, let me tell you all about the job."

"Okay."

"If they hire you, you'll be helping people fulfill their wishes. You would be working with a group of very good people that have been with the company for years. They're looking for someone exactly like you. Someone who has a good work history and good ethics. Someone they can trust and has no previous felonies. I take it; you don't?"

Chuckling, Mary Jane answered, "No, ma'am."

"Didn't think so," Mrs. Wilson said, grinning.

"Does it sound good so far?"

"Yes, ma'am."

"The rest may not, but trust me. I think if you remain open-minded and give it a chance, it'll work out nicely for you."

Mary Jane was very intrigued but worried at the same time. She wondered why Mrs. Wilson was beating around the bush. Was it that bad?

"One more thing. You would have to transfer. Are you willing to move?"

"I guess that depends on where?"

"Huntsville."

"As long as it's somewhere in Texas," Mary Jane answered, smiling.

"Now for the kicker. The position is with Huntsville State Penitentiary," she stated looking straight at Mary Jane, waiting for her response.

"Your office would be in a protected area away from prisoners, but you would be working with them. Do you want to hear more or does that completely turn you away?"

"I'm a bit unsure about it, but I still want to hear more, to be perfectly honest," she answered.

Smiling with approval, Mrs. Wilson continued, "I understand, dear, and appreciate your honesty. Your main duty, for this position, would be to fulfill last wishes for death row inmates, as well as managing all their affairs such as their last meal, family visits, sending and receiving mail, internet messages, and other similar responsibilities."

She stopped and waited for a response from the wide-eyed candidate.

"When I would be talking to the prisoners, would I be in the same room, right next to them?" Mary Jane slowly responded after thinking for a moment.

"Yes, but never alone, always with armed security, and the prisoners would always be restrained with hand and ankle cuffs," she answered reassuringly. "You would go through rigorous safety training so that you would know exactly how to stay safe. They wouldn't just throw you into the situation. There's a whole lot of state and federal regulations regarding safety."

"Oh, okay, as long as I felt safe, I would be very interested. It could be just the change I'm looking for. It's a bit scary, but very exciting at the same time."

"I'm so glad to hear you are willing to give it a try. I think it'll work out splendidly for you and them both. I'm going to call and set up an interview for you. Is that okay with you, dear?"

"Yes, ma'am."

"Remember what I told you in the beginning of our conversation. When you go to the interview, even if you're nervous, you're not going to let it show. What are you going to do?" she asked with a smile.

"Fake it till I make it," Mary Jane answered smiling back.

"It's very important that you don't let prisoners know if you're nervous. Always keep that in mind, dear," she said sincerely.

"Yes, ma'am. Thank you so much for everything."

"I'll call you when I have a date set up," she said with an odd grin, which Mary Jane wondered about as she walked to her car.

Chapter 7
The Good, the Bad, and the Ugly

As soon as Mary Jane left, Mrs. Wilson called the Huntsville state penitentiary.

"Hello, may I please speak to Mr. Wilson?"

"May I say who's calling, please?"

"Yes, this is his mother, Mrs. Wilson."

"Hold, please."

As she waited to speak to her son, she thought about how much she liked Mary Jane. For so long she had patiently waited for her son to find the right girl, marry, and give her some grandchildren. When he told her about the position at the penitentiary and asked her to fill it, she hoped that she would be able to kill two birds with one stone.

"Hi, Mom," he cheerfully answered.

"Hi, Jack."

"How are you doing, Mom?"

"Very well. How are you today?"

"Busy! I'm trying to do two jobs at once. But they're only paying me for one," he chuckled.

"Well then, you'll really enjoy what I'm about to tell you. I think I found the perfect girl for the job."

Excited, he answered, "Oh, great! Tell me about her."

"Well, she has a very stable work history, good ethics, and she's very family oriented."

"Is she hot?" he jokingly asked.

"Actually, she is. But I thought you didn't want me to set you up anymore."

"I know I said that, but I haven't been setting myself up very well here lately."

"Well, it's too late now. When you said not to, I gave up looking. You're on your own," she laughed, refusing to let him know that she did indeed set him up.

"Well, if she's hot, I might just hit on her anyway. How old is she, Mom?" he teased.

"Thirty-five, five years younger than you. I found her for the job, not for you," she said in the most serious voice she could muster.

"Does she have any experience with the prison system?"

"None at all, but she has had one employer since the age of sixteen, has good ethics and morals, and I really liked her a lot. She just seems to be a real good person."

"Okay, Mom, I trust your instincts. Did she say when she could interview?"

"She's available whenever you are."

"Sounds like my kinda girl," he teased. Little did he know the joke was on him.

"Haha. When would you like to interview her?" Mrs. Wilson asked as if she had no interest in his personal life.

"Well, let me look at my calendar," he said as he looked at his empty desk calendar. There was nothing but doodling all over it.

"Wow, I'm pretty booked up the rest of this month. But for you, I'll squeeze her in this week. Let's do it on Thursday."

"Oh, thank you, Son," she responded sarcastically. "I'll call her tomorrow and let her know."

"Okay, Mom, call me back and let me know if that's okay with her."

"Sure thing."

"I love you, Mom," he warmly ended their conversation.

"Love you too, Son."

℘ℭ

On Tuesday morning, as Mrs. Wilson prepared to call Mary Jane, she was hoping and praying that Mary Jane hadn't had nightmares about working with prisoners and had changed her mind.

Gertrude dialed and waited. Little did she know that, at that very moment, Mary Jane was waiting and hoping that Gertrude would call.

To Mary Jane's surprise, the phone rang just as she glanced at it willing it to ring. "Fake it till you make it," persisted in her thoughts.

"Hello," she answered, determined to sound confident.

"Hello, dear, this is Gertrude Wilson. How are you doing today?"

"Great! How are you, Mrs. Wilson?"

"Great, as well. But please call me Gertrude," she asked.

"Gertrude it is," Mary Jane giggled.

"I have good news for you, dear. I spoke with the warden at Huntsville and told him all about you. He's very interested and would like to know if you're available this Thursday for an interview."

"I'm off this Thursday, so that would be perfect. That was surprisingly fast."

"Oh, yes, I agree. They're very anxious to fill the position."

"Gertrude, I feel very comfortable with you—almost like

family. I want to thank you for everything—your advice, your kindness, and your time."

"That's very sweet of you. I just want you to know that I think you're a very special young lady, and I wish you the best."

"Thank you! Can I ask you something personal?"

"Sure."

"What do you think I should wear to the interview? I have no idea what to wear to prison," she laughed.

Laughing with her, Gertrude answered, "That is a good question. I hear the warden is single and about your age, so I would go with something professional, yet a little sexy."

"Sounds like I better go shopping," Mary Jane agreed, thinking how funny it sounded for an older woman to suggest dressing sexy.

ô•ô

Thursday morning arrived, and Mary Jane first went to an appointment for professional makeup and hairstyling. She had decided that she was going to go in with a bang and knock the warden's socks off. Then, she would decide if she wanted the job, not the other way around. After hair and makeup, she went to get her nails done. Then, she went home and put on her new, sexy, black, low-cut business dress and black high heels. She stepped back and looked at herself in the full-length mirror on the bathroom door.

"Wow, I already know I have the job if I want it," she said admiring herself. She slid on the sexy jacket, grabbed her new black handbag, and started to head out the door as she remembered Mrs. Wilson. She wished she could see her now. So, she grabbed her cell phone, took a picture of herself in the full-length mirror, and sent it to Mrs. Wilson via email.

As Mary Jane drove down the freeway towards Huntsville, her phone buzzed with a new message. She looked down at it, and it was a picture Mrs. Wilson had taken of herself with a big smile on her face. Mary Jane felt like she had a new friend. On the other end, Mrs. Wilson felt the same, and secretly, she also hoped that Mary Jane was her future daughter-in-law with grandchildren in the making.

As Mary Jane neared the prison, she could see how enormous and intimidating it actually was. It was surrounded by an enormous brick wall laden with, what looked to be, razor-sharp wires. Once she reached the entrance, a security guard motioned for her to stop. She rolled down the car window and explained to the officer that she was there to see Mr. Wilson. As Mary Jane waited, the guard called Mr. Wilson for approval and thoroughly inspected her car inside and out. He also asked Mary Jane if she had any weapons on herself or inside the vehicle. Feeling sweat bead up on her forehead, she wanted to reach for a tissue but was too afraid. Finally, he gave Mary Jane instructions as to which building to meet the warden. Once inside and parked at the correct building, she could see that there were more internal walled barriers. She was relieved until she noticed a guard leading a line of prisoners in shackles down a nearby sidewalk. She didn't dare move until they were further away. As she watched, they got closer and closer instead of further away as she had hoped. Then, she noticed that the sidewalk ran right in front of her parking spot.

She sat frozen as the shackled men passed right in front of her, staring at her as they were escorted by. Several of them puckered their lips and blew kisses at her. Some smiled at her with missing teeth, and some just stared at her with an empty, lifeless face, which she liked the least. She wondered what they were thinking. She couldn't help but stare back as a group of about twenty filed by. She searched the premises to make sure the coast was clear, and there were no more chain gangs approaching before she stepped out from the safety of her car.

There was another guard at the entrance to the building, who questioned and searched her before she was allowed to enter. She was relieved that he was polite and professional and didn't touch what he shouldn't. Sweat had beaded on her forehead again. So once inside, she looked for a bathroom to freshen up. Spotting one, she stepped inside, went immediately into a stall, and quickly locked the door as if it were protecting her from the outside. Leaning on the stall door, she took a deep breath and said to herself, "You can do this."

"Are you talking to me?" Mary Jane heard another voice say from the next stall.

Embarrassed, she answered, "No, I didn't know anyone else was in here. Sorry, I'm a bit nervous."

"That's ok. Is there anything I can help you with?" said the voice.

"Maybe. I have an interview with Mr. Wilson," she said as she walked out of the stall and toward the mirror. "Do you know where his office is?"

Giggling, Isabella answered, "Yes, I can take you there."

"I guess that was a silly question," Mary Jane responded. "He is the warden. I'm sure everyone here knows where his office is."

Isabella stepped out of the stall, and they eyed each other in the mirror as Mary Jane applied her lipstick.

"Don't worry about it. Interviews are always nerve-racking. I'm Isabella, by the way, Mr. Wilson's secretary," she said as she extended her hand.

Shaking her hand, Mary Jane introduced herself.

"Oh, great! If anybody knows where his office is, you should," Mary Jane said with a nervous chuckle.

"Don't worry, he's really nice," she reassured. "Besides, you look fantastic, and you seem really nice too. I guarantee, he's going to like you." Smiling, Isabella locked arms with Mary Jane and said, "Come on, I'll take you there."

Isabella's friendly gestures made Mary Jane feel much better, and she was able to relax a bit as they made their way down the hall.

Isabella knocked and entered the warden's office with Mary Jane following. Taken by her beauty, Warden Wilson stood up immediately.

Noticing his reaction, Isabella could barely contain her laughter but politely said, "Jack, this is Mary Jane Scarsdale. She's here for the interview, right on time."

As he walked around the desk, his eyes remained fixed on Mary Jane.

As he approached, he did not extend his hand. Instead, put his hand on her shoulder and gently led her to the chair in front of his enormous desk, "Hi, Ms. Scarsdale. I'm Jack Wilson. I know you had a long drive. What can I get for you to drink?"

"Oh, I'm fine," she answered barely able to think about anything besides how handsome he was, and how strong and sexy his hand felt on her shoulder.

"No, I want you to feel comfortable while you're here. Do you drink coffee?"

"Coffee actually does sound good."

"How would you like it?" As the words rolled out of his mouth, he thought how inappropriate the question sounded. But at the same time, wondered how she did like it.

She didn't mean too, but she did take the question inappropriately and thought, *with you on top.*

"Pretty creamy with one teaspoon of sugar," she answered blushing while trying to tame her nasty thoughts.

"Isabella, can you please get both of us a cup of coffee?"

"I'm on it. Anything else?" she asked while watching both of their faces turn red.

"Can you please bring Mary Jane's file?" he asked wanting to pull himself together.

"Yes, sir."

Wide-eyed, Mary Jane asked, "I have a file?"

"Unfortunately, in these days and times, everyone is under

scrutiny," he stated as he sat down opposite her. "Everyone here has been carefully selected—especially me. They're constantly keeping an eye on me," he said smiling at her with a devilish smile that made Mary Jane's heart flutter.

"Well, tell me, what do you think about our place so far? Being from Alvin, I know this is probably pretty intimidating."

"Well, yeah, it is."

"It's okay. Believe me, I understand. I was even intimidated when I first came here. And sometimes, if I think about it too much, I still get nervous. That's what keeps us on our toes."

Isabella placed the folder in front of Mr. Wilson and gave each of them a mug of coffee.

He opened the folder and politely said, "Go ahead, enjoy your coffee. I'm going to take a quick peek at your folder."

Isabella had never seen Jack that nervous. She knew he had already looked through Mary Jane's folder and knew everything about her.

His mother did say Mary Jane was hot. But he wasn't prepared for drop dead beautiful. He now suspected that his mother had sent him a potential grandchild generator. He couldn't count the times his mother had tried to set him up. He told her time and time again that he didn't want to settle down and have to answer to anyone. He had done that before and grew quite disgusted with it. The girl he dated through high school and into his twenties watched everything he did and ridiculed it, giving him issues for many years. It took Jack's psychiatrist two years and several different medications to pull him out of the depression and insecurity. He wasn't going to let that happen again. Instead, Jack built an enormous wall around himself—much like the one he worked in, around the prison. Even so, girls were always after Jack because he was very attractive, smart, funny, and charmingly elusive.

Dating was only for sex, as far as Jack was concerned. For almost twenty years, he had not dated one girl for more than six months at a time. That's about the time they always started talking about love and marriage. That's when Jack made his exit. Besides, he loved to fish and called the ocean his "lady." Spending all of his money and time on his Boston Whaler, the *Captain Jack*, seemed like a better alternative to him.

As he pretended to look in her folder, Jack told himself not to give into his mother's tricks but knew he would.

Looking up, he said with a friendly smile, "I'll get right to the point. You come highly recommended by my mother's hiring agency. I really like that you have perseverance and have stayed with one job for nineteen years. Not only that, they seem to appreciate you very much. When my mother called The Golden Skillet, they had nothing but nice things to say about you. The agency and I believe you're a good fit here, but I want to make sure you're going to feel comfortable, as well. It can be overwhelming. Did my mother explain what your duties would be?" he asked and paused for her response. He couldn't help but notice a strange look of confusion on her face.

All Mary Jane heard out of everything he said was, "his mother's agency." Who was his mother? Was Mrs. Wilson his mother? She thought the same last name was just coincidental.

"Is everything okay, Ms. Scarsdale?" he finally asked.

"If you don't mind me asking, who is your mother?"

"Mrs. Wilson, the lady that interviewed you."

Amazed and confused, she responded, "I wonder why she didn't tell me."

Something was not quite right about this situation, but she didn't have time to digest it and figure it out. She would think about it on the long drive home.

"Yeah, I wonder why she didn't." Not wanting to be even more embarrassed than he already was, he pretended not to know.

Changing the subject, he said, "How about this? We can talk as I give you a grand tour. I'll show you where your office would be and every place that you would travel while you're here—give you the good, the bad, and the ugly. Then, you can think on it and give me a callback."

"I would like that very much," she said with a reassuring smile.

She tried very hard to put the mother issue to rest so that she could focus on making a good decision.

He rose first and said, "Your office would be right down the hall from mine. We'll go there first."

"Oh, well, I feel very safe here close to you," she said a little flirty.

He noticed and walked with his shoulders just a bit higher.

He stopped only four doors down. The door was made of some magnificent wood just like his. He opened it for her, smiled, and said, "Come on in."

Wide-eyed, she stepped in. Her eyes first went to the enormous desk. "That is a beautiful desk. What kind of wood is that?"

"It's mahogany. All the wood in my office and all the wood in this one is mahogany. This was my office when I first started here, and I fixed it up like this. Then, when I moved to the other office, I decorated it the same way. I guess you can tell; I really like mahogany."

The mahogany bookshelves lined the back wall from ceiling to floor. A black leather, high-back executive chair sat between the shelves and the mahogany desk. On the back wall, to the outside of the shelves, were two slender windows that ran from near the ceiling almost all the way to the floor, allowing in plenty of sunshine.

Mary Jane's eyes were wandering through the room in amazement.

"Do you like it? If you don't, we can change it around for you."

Turning around and smiling at Jack, Mary Jane said, "I love it. I wouldn't change a thing."

"Great! Let's continue on our tour, shall we?" He said as he gestured for her to go first.

"You've seen the good. Now comes the bad and the ugly."

He led her back to his office where he made a phone call.

"Is the interrogation room available? Ok, we are on the way. Make sure the area is secure. I have a female interviewee with me," she heard him say. As he hung up, he reassured Mary Jane, "You should always phone ahead and do the same thing I just did before proceeding through the secured doors. Our officers are very protective of our staff here."

"That's very reassuring," admitted Mary Jane. As they walked down the long corridor, Jack asked, "Did my mother tell you what your duties would be here?"

"She said I would be helping death row inmates fulfill their last requests."

"Yes, you would be doing that. You would also be working with other high-security inmates—helping them with general things like communication with their families, attorneys, stuff like that," he explained.

At the end of the hall, he stopped at a door and looked through its thick glass pane before motioning for security to unlock it.

"I'll enter first, and you follow me," he instructed her.

"Okay," said Mary Jane calmly. She felt safe with Jack Wilson. Otherwise, she would have been terrified at that moment.

As she stepped through the door, she saw tiny rooms down each side of a small walkway. Each room was made transparent with glass walls. In the center of the tiny rooms, was another glass wall separating it into two halves.

"This is the visitation area. The prisoners have visitation on Saturdays and Sundays."

They walked down the compact hallway into a larger area with rooms all along its perimeter. On the door to one of the rooms was written, "Interrogation."

"This is where you'll be doing most of the visiting with your clientele. Or, you can have a guard bring them to your office if you're more comfortable there," he said as he gestured her to enter first.

Inside were only four items: one long conference table and three wooden chairs.

"This is the ugly." He pointed to a glassed wall. "That's a two way. When you're talking to an inmate in here, there'll always be an officer with you, along with another one on the other side of that glass. The inmate will always be cuffed at the wrists and the ankles. Plus, if you choose to conference in here, you can video."

"Are you ready to see the bad?"

"I guess so."

"Don't worry; we aren't going to get close to them. You'll be able to see them, but they won't see you," Jack said. "Don't take this the wrong way, but you're gorgeous and they, well, they haven't been with a woman for a while."

Blushing, she said, "Thank you for the compliment."

Once he saw she was okay with flattery, he laid it on a bit thicker.

"If I were your boyfriend, I wouldn't want them seeing you looking that good," he flirted.

Feeling embarrassed, she redirected the conversation.

"Thank you! That leads me to a question."

"Shoot," he responded, feeling that he overdid it.

"If we both decide this is a good fit for me, what should I wear every day?"

"Oh, we have standardized uniforms for all personnel."

He wanted to tell her that she would look cute in that too but refrained.

"Oh good, that makes it easy."

"I do have a few more questions now," she said looking at him waiting for a cue.

"Okay, let's get back to my office, and discuss it over another cup of coffee," he said with a happy smile.

"All right."

Since both of their minds were preoccupied with each other, they both forgot the rest of the tour. She was never shown, what Jack referred to as, "the bad."

Coffee in hand and sitting in Jack's comfortable office, Mary Jane initiated the conversation. "The two things I'm really curious about is why the death row inmates get last wishes and what sort of things do they wish for?"

Smiling and nodding his head yes in agreement, he answered, "I often wonder why they get last wishes also. It seems criminals have all the rights and protection these days. It's not like it was before. I prefer the days when they were hung on a tree for the whole town to see. It definitely irks me that some guy who raped and killed some poor little girl gets anything but hung by a splintered rope. As far as what they wish for, some ask to see their kids one last time, some for a certain meal, and some don't want anything. And of course, you get crazy requests that just can't be fulfilled—like a day of freedom."

"How will I know if I can grant their wish or not?"

"Don't worry about that. You'll be getting plenty of training. And if you have any questions, you can always ask me."

"Okay, I'm definitely interested in trying this out. I just have a few worries about being able to do a good job."

"That's good. That shows you care. I'm actually glad to hear that. As far as I'm concerned, the job's yours, but I have to run your paperwork through the obstacle course first. I'm sure that won't be any problem," Jack assured her.

"Great," she responded with a big smile. "I really am very excited."

"I think you'll do a great job here," Jack said as he smiled back.

They finished their conversation, and Jack walked Mary Jane to her car. Most of Jack's conversations ended up turning into fishing stories, and this one was no different. By the time they reached the car, he had told her all about last weekend's great fishing trip.

"I love to fish!" exclaimed Mary Jane. "We had a beach house growing up, and my dad always took me fishing with him."

"Get outta here! Don't tell me you can bait your own hook too."

"Of course, I can."

"You'll have to prove that to me. I don't believe it. You're a girly girl, aren't you?" he chided.

Shaking her head at him, she said, "I can do anything you can do when it comes to fishing—probably even better," she challenged.

"That sounds like a direct challenge to me. I'm going fishing this weekend. The weather's supposed to be perfect, and the seas are only gonna be one-foot rollers. Why don't you go with me?"

"I would love to. I haven't been in fifteen or twenty years."

"And, in roll the excuses," he laughed.

"No, no excuses. But I may need a few tips from a professional such as yourself," she teased.

"Okay, I have your phone number. Mind if I use it to set up our competition?"

"I wouldn't mind if you called me anytime you wanted," she flirted.

Smiling ear to ear, Jack responded, "I'm gonna take you up on that."

Mary Jane climbed into her car as Jack opened the door for her.

"Buckle up and be safe. You have a long drive. Why don't you go ahead and call me when you get there, so I'll know you made it home okay," Jack said as he leaned over and into her window. Mary Jane was wanting him to kiss her but knew it was way too soon for that.

"I don't have your number," Mary Jane said softly.

"I can take care of that," he said as he took his phone out. "What's your phone number?"

As soon as she told him her number, he dialed it and said, "Now you have it. Call me anytime. The more often, the better," he said smiling down at her.

"Okay, let me save it before I leave," Mary Jane said sweetly.

Jack wanted to kiss her before she left, but he, too, knew it was too soon.

As she drove away, she watched Jack in her rearview mirror. He watched her until she turned the corner and was out of sight.

"Oh, my God," said Mary Jane out loud. "He is such a hunk."

She picked up her phone quickly to make sure she had hung up earlier. She was elated. She didn't know if she was more excited about Jack or the new position.

"What's the deal with his Mom?" She suddenly remembered. "Why did she not tell me she was his mom? Hmm, I wonder if she asked me all those personal questions to find out if I was daughter-in-law material. I think I may have been framed." she laughed. "It's okay, but I can't believe she did that. Do you want to have children? I should have known. That has nothing to do with that job. She is amazingly smooth. I really like her, and she must really like me," she conversed out loud to herself.

ॐ

Jack smiled all the way back to his office and decided to call his mother and thank her.

"Hello," answered Mrs. Wilson.

"Hello, Mom. I know what you did, Mom."

"What did I do?" she asked innocently.

"Oh, come on. You send over an incredibly gorgeous, intelligent, single young lady for me to interview. Knowing you, you told her to dress like that."

"Like what?"

"Well, she was dressed very nice and professional, but pretty darn sexy too."

"Well instead of fussing at me, tell me, do you think she would make a good executer?"

"Actually, I think she has great qualifications. Did you search high and low for her, or did she just stumble into your lap?"

"She called the agency. I was just an innocent bystander."

"Well, I guess the proper thing to do here is say—are you ready for this? Thanks, Mom!"

"Wait, hold on a minute while I pick myself up off the floor," she laughed.

"Mom, all kidding aside. She's amazing. She wants to try the job out, plus we have a fishing trip set up."

"Oh, my gosh! Y'alls first date is fishing?"

"What better place is there?" he chuckled knowing his Mom would have arranged a whole different setting.

"Jack, does she even like to fish?"

"I'm surprised you didn't ask her."

"Well, I didn't think that fishing was a prerequisite for an executer."

Laughing hard, Jack said, "You're never going to admit it, are you?"

"I don't know what you're talking about," she refused to admit anything.

Jack looked out his window at the setting sun and all the brilliant colors of the sky as they finished their conversation. He was thinking that there isn't a better place for a first date than on the peaceful water with a beautiful sunset like that.

Chapter 8
The Competition

As Jack attempted to back the boat down the ramp, Mary Jane stretched out at the end of the pier and soaked up the warm rays of the sun. As she lay back, propped on her elbows, her long red hair was flying in the Gulf breeze, and her firm body was illuminated by the sunshine. She loved to feel the sun's warmth on her skin. Often, she would sunbathe out by the pool at her apartment. And, even though she was redheaded, she had obtained a rich, golden tan. As Mary Jane slumbered at the end of the dock in her new swimsuit, she spotted Jack's reflection in his rearview mirror. He was smiling ear to ear and looking directly at her. She began laughing as she watched the boat zigzag back and forth until it finally reached the water.

Once he finally got the boat into the water, he walked down the pier toward Mary Jane.

"I'm usually very good at that, but I had something in my eye," confessed Jack.

"I know. I saw your reflection in the mirror. Sorry about that," laughed Mary Jane.

"You have nothing to be sorry about," smiled Jack.

"Can you hold the boat to the dock while I park the truck?" he asked still smiling ear to ear.

"Good luck," she replied as she took the rope from his hand.

As he walked away, he turned to get another look at Mary Jane. Smiling, he turned to see her smiling back at him.

By the time he made it back to the boat, Mary Jane had the boat tied to the dock and the two motors started.

Laughing, he said, "Now you're scaring me. Maybe you do know what you're doing. But I hope you know; I can't let you out fish me."

"After watching you back the boat down the ramp, I'm quite confident I can," she teased.

"Well, I'm telling you, I've never had that much trouble before. You're a beautiful distraction," he flirted.

Mary Jane sat on the seat next to Jack as he drove the boat to his special spot. As he stood next to her with his hand on the throttle, he was having a hard time keeping his eyes on the water and not her. Out of the corner of his eye, he watched Mary Jane. He wanted, so badly, to put his hand on her leg, but knew it was too soon.

"So how often do you work out?" loudly asked Jack over the roar of the motors.

"Oh, you can tell?" modestly asked Mary Jane, even though she was quite confident and knew that he hadn't been able to take his eyes off of her.

"Yeah, you look great!" answered Jack.

"Thanks, so do you. Do you work out?" asked Mary Jane.

Exaggerating a bit, Jack answered, "Yeah, a little, but obviously not as much as you do. Do you watch everything you eat too?" he asked.

"No, I love to eat! That's why I work out," she laughed.

"Good, I love a girl that's not afraid to eat. Do you drink?"

"When I was younger, I drank a lot. Now that I've gotten older, I'll have a few drinks, but not enough to get falling down drunk."

"What do you like to drink?" he asked.

"Rum is my favorite."

Smiling, he said, "That's my favorite, too."

He slowed the boat down and asked, "Would you like one now?"

"I would love one."

Jack made each one of them a rum and coke on ice in a red solo cup and continued on to the spot.

After she finished that one drink, she said, "That sure did taste good out here on the water. I've never drank on the water before. Last time I went fishing, I was too young to drink."

"Would you like another?"

Liquid courage took over her thoughts and emotions, and she asked, "Are you going to try to take advantage of me?"

"Do you want me to?" he asked, looking very sexy to Mary Jane.

"Maybe," she answered.

"Well, the first drink was free, but another will cost ya," he said

"What will it cost?" asked Mary Jane, willing to play along.

"Just one kiss," he answered looking into her eyes for a response.

"Well, I really want another drink, so maybe you should slow the boat down so I can pay you first."

Without a moment's hesitation, Jack grabbed the throttle and slowed the boat to a stop.

As he stood next to her, he turned and leaned toward Mary Jane and kissed her gently on the lips. Per the deal, he started to pull away after the one kiss. But Mary Jane placed her hand on the back of his head and pulled him back. Gently, yet seductively, she ran her tongue along his bottom lip and then softly in toward his tongue. Jack had no problem responding. He always prided himself on being a great kisser. He knew what women liked—or so he thought. He let her have control of his tongue as she sucked it in and out of hers. He rubbed the tops of her firm legs and wanted to rub her inner thigh, but wasn't sure she was ready for him to. Her hands freely roamed all over his chest and his wide, hard shoulders. He had her favorite type of body. A triangle she called it—wide at the shoulders and slimming toward the abdomen and butt.

Mary Jane and Jack became very aroused within minutes, and they both felt it was time to slow things down.

"Am I paid in full?" she asked Jack as she pulled her lips away from his.

Barely able to speak, in a low, weak voice which he didn't recognize, he answered, "That pays for all the liquor on the boat."

Jack made them another drink at the cooler in the back of the boat. From the seat, Mary Jane turned around to watch him. As he kept looking up smiling at her, he spilled one of the drinks. Both of them started laughing, which made him spill more. Finally, the drinks were made, and they were underway once again.

Jack pulled up to the spot he had saved on his GPS and turned on the depth finder. He pointed to the screen, "See all the fish?"

"Those are all fish?" she asked with excitement. "We didn't have anything that sophisticated when I last went fishing."

"I know, isn't it great?" he enthusiastically responded.

She could see how much he loved fishing as he happily rigged two poles—one for him and one for her.

"So what you're going to do is drop down until you hit bottom, then reel up a couple of times to get it off the bottom. Otherwise, they'll get you down into the wreck, and you'll never get 'em up."

"Oh, there's a wreck down there?" she asked.

"Yep, a friend of mine gave me these numbers. It's a great spot."

He put a fighting belt on Mary Jane and handed her the pole and the live beeliner they caught at the last buoy.

He smiled at her and asked, "Are you sure you want to bait

your own hook?"

"We didn't use live bait. Just show me where to run the hook through," she said determined to do it on her own.

"What did y'all use?" he asked.

"Shrimp and squid from what I can remember."

He grabbed his pole and another live bait and said, "Like this," as he ran the hook through the top of the bait.

"Like this?" she asked as she did the same.

"Perfect," he smiled. "I've always wanted a girl that could bait her own hook."

Proudly, she smiled. She already wanted to be everything Jack ever desired.

She dropped her line down to the bottom and reeled up a couple of times just as Jack had instructed.

No sooner than she reeled up a couple of times, she felt something hit her bait and started trying to pull her line down. Leaning back with the pole, she started fighting the fish.

"Pull up, reel down," Jack coached with excitement.

"What do you mean? Show me," Mary Jane squealed as the fish was getting the better of her.

He stood behind her with his loins pushed into her backside and placed his hands on the pole above hers.

"Pull back," he instructed as he helped pull the pole back. "And reel down," he said as he slowly let her rod go down while she reeled.

"Like this?" she asked as she reeled on the way down and then pulled the pole back up.

"Exactly! Now you've got it. Go get 'em, girl," he cheered.

"Pull back, reel down. You're doing perfect. You're a natural," he coached.

She muscled the fish all the way up as her arms throbbed, but she refused to show any weakness by reeling slower. Jack was astonished at the size of the fish when it got to the top of the water. He grabbed the gaff, hooked it under the fins, and pulled it into the boat.

"What kind of fish is that? It's kind of ugly," asked Mary Jane.

"It's a grouper. Ugly is in the eye of the beholder," responded Jack.

"I have to tell ya; I'm completely surprised that a beautiful girl like you just muscled a fish in like that. I am very impressed."

Loving his compliments, she was smiling ear to ear.

He quickly grabbed the camera. Then, he showed her how to hold the fish out toward the camera which makes it look enormous and took pictures. After he had taken a couple of shots, his reel started singing. He rushed over, grabbed his pole, and reeled in another grouper. It didn't take him near the time to reel in his fish. Mary Jane didn't care about the timing near as much as she cared about the size of the fish. To Mary Jane's disappointment, his grouper was obviously bigger than hers. Eager to win the fishing competition, she wanted to drop back down and catch a bigger one than his. Jack had other intentions. He decided he would really get her goat.

"We're going to another spot. I don't want to overfish this area," he said with a devilish smile.

"No way! I can't believe that you're going to be like that!" squealed Mary Jane in disbelief.

"It's the right thing to do," proudly smiled Jack.

Mary Jane was loving the fun competition between them.

"This is not over," she promised with a smile.

By the end of the day, Mary Jane was still left in second place, and Jack had the biggest catch.

On the way home, instead of sitting in the passenger seat, as she did on the way down, she snuggled up next to Jack.

Jack was deeply infatuated with Mary Jane, and her with him, but it was too soon for either of them to admit.

"Has Anabelle called and set up your orientation yet?" Jack asked.

"Yes, she did. I start in two weeks. Monday, I have to give my two-week notice at the restaurant."

"That means in two weeks, I get to see you every day," he said while thinking that he didn't want to wait two weeks before he saw her again.

"Yeah, I'm so glad you're there. I have to tell you; I feel very safe with you."

"That's one of the nicest things you could say to me. That's really very important to me."

"Good, then you'll like this too. Earlier, I was thinking about when I was a little girl, and we went fishing. I always knew my Dad would get us back in safe. I fully trusted him. Until now, I haven't felt that safe with anyone. When we were out on the boat today, I knew that you were fully capable of handling any situation that came along, and you would get us back in safe and sound."

"Wow! I'm glad I make you feel that way. Honestly, I would do whatever it took to keep you safe."

"I know. I can see and feel that about you. I know I haven't known you very long, but I can see that you're a real good man, Jack."

"Since we're passing out compliments, let me just say, that I think you're a real good girl. They don't make good girls like you anymore."

"That's because good girls aren't in demand, Jack," she laughed.

"Well, I have to disagree with that. I'd like one."

"Well, if you play your cards right, maybe you can have one," she teased.

"Speaking of cards, do you like to hit the casinos?" he inquired, thinking he had found a way to see her again.

"I do. The whole time I was growing up, my dad had a poker night. He and his buddies taught me how to play."

"Your dad sounds awesome. He taught you to do a lot didn't he?"

"Yeah, he did. Do you like to play cards, too?"

"At the casino," stated Jack.

"I haven't played too many cards at the casino," admitted Mary Jane.

"Well, how about if we go this next weekend? I've been wanting to try out L'Auberge in Lake Charles."

"That sounds fun."

"So it's a date?" boyishly asked Jack.

"Yes. Which day this weekend are we talking about?" she inquired.

"Well, the thing is, it's pretty far for me, so we need to stay the night. I promise to be a good boy," he said as he innocently tapped her leg.

"Okay, we can do that," she said sweetly, but she thought that she wasn't sure if she could spend the night with him and maintain a good girl status.

ഇ ഌ

From that day forward, they spoke to each other on the phone every day. Throughout the week, they were both looking forward to the weekend at the casino together. As the weekend neared, Mary Jane prepared for the trip. She shaved her legs and packed her sexiest undergarments—just in case.

Jack, in preparation, shaved his face and packed his newest Fruit of the Looms without holes.

Saturday finally arrived, and Jack and Mary Jane headed for Louisiana. They had great fun playing cards and slots all day.

Saturday night, they had a great steak dinner, several rum and cokes, laughter, and great conversation. Then, they went to their plush room. The moment they entered the room, they laid on the bed and started kissing and caressing one another.

Mary Jane whispered seductively in Jack's ear, "I want you so bad right now." Jack was really planning on being a gentleman, but not if she gave the slightest invitation, and that was it.

Within moments they had taken each other's clothes off.

"What do you want, Jack?" She knew men loved hearing their names in bed.

"I want you, Mary Jane," he said as he flipped her over, repositioning her beneath him. "You're so beautiful," he said, as he passionately looked into her eyes.

After the intimate encounter, the two lay embracing each other when Mary Jane declared, "I have to be honest with you. I don't have recreational sex, and I don't share. If you want to be with me, you can't be with anyone else."

"I completely agree. I don't want anyone else to have you either."

Jack loved her boldness. In fact, he loved everything about her.

Soon, they fell asleep in each other's arms. Jack awoke and looked over at Mary Jane, who was lying wide awake.

"Good morning, Beautiful," Jack whispered in her ear.

"Good morning, Handsome," Mary Jane responded.

"Guess what?" Jack asked.

"What?" answered Mary Jane, imagining that he was going to say something romantic.

"I'm really hungry," Jack stated.

"Me too," she agreed.

"You know what sounds good?" he asked.

"What?"

"Cheesecake."

"That sounds sinfully delicious. Cheesecake at two in the morning after a romp in the hay," she giggled.

"I'm glad you agree. Let's go get it," Jack said as he was getting dressed.

They went downstairs and sat at a little table for two and shared a piece of cheesecake at two in the morning.

"This is the best cheesecake I've ever had," she admitted.

"I think I know why," smiled Jack.

Even though they didn't win any money gambling, they left the casino with smiles on their faces.

"I have been having the best time with you. I'm crazy about you, Jack," Mary Jane confessed on their drive back home. Jack turned and looked at her and said, "I'm crazy about you too, Mary Jane."

Surprising to Jack, he wasn't one bit afraid of Mary Jane. For a change, he didn't feel as though he were being trapped.

Chapter 9
Mrs. Walking Dead

Mary Jane was relieved to know she had a knight in shining armor at the prison. Otherwise, she wasn't so sure she would have accepted the position. She knew that she could count on Jack for anything she needed. Surprisingly, she wasn't worried about her safety as much as she was worried about disappointing Jack and her new fellow employees.

As she neared the prison, her cell phone rang.

"Hello," she answered.

"Good morning, Beautiful!" Jack happily answered.

With a smile, Mary Jane responded, "Good morning."

"Are you almost here?" asked Jack.

"Right down the street," responded Mary Jane.

"Great! I'm going to meet you in the parking lot and walk you in."

"That would be great! Thank you!"

Moments later, they both tried to look professional as they walked next to each other, without any hint of romance. It felt unnatural to both of them as they walked down the hall toward her new office.

"I have a surprise for you," he proudly announced.

"What is it?" she asked with excitement.

"Look," he said as he pointed to her office door.

"Mary Jane Scarsdale" in bold, black print over a gold nameplate was already in place on the door.

Delighted, she squealed, "How sweet of you, Jack."

"There's more," he added. "Look inside."

He opened the door as she stepped inside. On the enormous mahogany desk sat a golden nameplate with her name engraved on it. Next to the nameplate was a beautiful bouquet of red roses. Without a second of hesitation, she turned and shut the door behind them, pushed Jack against the door with her body and gave him a luscious kiss for his kindness.

"Jack, you're the sweetest man I've ever known. Thank you so much!"

Smiling ear to ear, Jack said, "You're welcome."

Suddenly, there was a knock at the door. In response, they quickly stepped away from each other.

"Sorry, wasn't sure where y'all were," said Isabella as she quickly entered the office. "The general orientation is about to begin in five minutes right down the hall," she said suspiciously looking back and forth between the flowers and Jack. Neither Jack nor Mary Jane uttered a word, and both looked as though they were caught with their hand in the cookie jar.

Obviously distracted, Isabella said, "We better get going, Mary Jane. I'll walk you. Again, welcome to Huntsville. Let me know if you need anything."

Shaking her head and frowning at Jack, Isabella walked out while motioning for Mary Jane to follow. In the hall, Isabella had to ask, "Is he hitting on you already?"

Unsure that she should confide in Isabella, Mary Jane quickly decided to answer honestly, "We've been seeing each other."

"I'm going to tell you flat out, I like you, Mary Jane. You seem like a real nice lady, so I'm going to be honest with you. I like Jack, too, but he's a bit of a playboy, and he knows I'm going to say something to you. Jack and I have worked together for ten years here, and we know each other very well. Like I said, he's a great guy. He just has a problem committing. Don't let him hurt you, Mary Jane," she finished as Jack peered down the hallway to see if Isabella was telling Mary Jane what a dog he was.

"Well, I kind of figured that when he told me how old he was and had never been married, he either had to be a playboy or gay. Now, thanks to you, the mystery is solved—playboy it is," giggled Mary Jane trying to lighten the conversation.

"Don't say I didn't warn you," concluded Isabella.

"Thanks for caring, Isabella. I promise I'll be careful."

Jack knew that Isabella would warn Mary Jane and hoped that whatever she said about him wouldn't make Mary Jane leery. As Mary Jane sat through orientation, Jack worried.

Finally, at 5 p.m., the work day ended, and Mary Jane was exhausted from orientation. Jack convinced her to stay with him so that she wouldn't have to drive all the way back to Alvin. To his relief, she gladly accepted the offer.

"How would you like some fresh grouper for dinner?" asked Jack as they drove down the highway toward his house.

"That sounds so good. I'm really hungry. Jack, I have to ask you something."

"I already know," he sighed. "Let me just tell you now. I have dated a lot of women, and I didn't want to settle down with any of them. One of the biggest reasons is that I let an old girlfriend mess me up, and I had to see a shrink for two years because of it. So, I'm very careful who I turn my heart over to. I don't think that's necessarily a bad thing—to be careful with your heart," he turned to look at Mary Jane hoping for understanding.

"I was just going to ask if you had some wine at your house," she laughed.

Jack heartily laughed with her, and responded, "No, but we can stop and get some."

Mary Jane was glad Jack confided in her and said, "Jack, I

understand. I'm in the same boat you're in. I haven't settled down either."

Jack was relieved to see Mary Jane understood and wasn't apprehensive about him. To convince him that she wasn't concerned, Mary Jane scooted closer to him and placed her hand on his leg.

Being single for a long time taught her something that couldn't be learned from a book. She knew about the psychology of a scared heart, and she had no problem giving Jack all the space he needed. Besides, she was in no hurry either. They talked all the rest of the way home about their day, but not about their unsuccessful past relationships. Neither of them ever planned on bringing the subject up again. All she wanted to do was to enjoy the relationship that she and Jack had. She refused to worry about his past.

Jack cooked the grouper they had caught on their fishing trip. They ate the fresh fish, drank wine, and talked and talked. There were no awkward moments of silence. Both remarked about feeling like they had been together for a long time and were very comfortable with each other. As they sat comfortably snuggled up on the couch, Jack revealed to Mary Jane how he felt for her.

"Mary Jane I'm not trying to scare you away, but I really like you—a lot. I feel that we are meant to be together and wish we would have met a long time ago."

Laughing, Mary Jane sweetly answered, "You can't scare me away. I really like you a lot too, Jack."

∽∾

For two weeks, Mary Jane stayed with Jack while attending orientation. On her last day of orientation, which was Friday, Mary Jane decided she should go home for the weekend to catch up on chores and visit her parents, Earl and Marjorie.

In between romantic phone conversations, most of Mary Janes's weekend was spent doing laundry and cleaning up two weeks' worth of dust. She was only able to spend a few hours on Saturday with her parents. Her mom made her favorite meal of roast, potatoes, and carrots which were fresh from the garden. For dessert, they had home-made apple pie which had always been the family's favorite dessert—probably because the apples were right out of their own backyard. They had five apple trees that produced so many apples that, each year, her mom canned enough to last several years. After their food fest, Mary Jane said her goodbyes, and the rest of the weekend quickly flew by. Before she knew it, Monday morning arrived, and she was on her way back to Huntsville.

As she pulled into the parking area of the prison, she spotted Jack shyly waiting to walk her in.

"Don't you think you're being a bit obvious," she grinned.

"I'm the king here and can date any wench I choose," he grinned back.

"Wench? Watch it, King Jack,"

"Whoops, did I go too far?"

"Yes, how will you make up for it?" she smiled mischievously.

"How about if I wine and dine you to celebrate your first day?"

"Add a massage to that, and you have a deal."

"I will trump that. I will wine and dine you, give you a massage, and a place to sleep," he said proudly.

"Okay, I guess I can forgive you then," she shrugged.

As she walked into her new office, she saw her wilted red roses sitting on the top bookshelf and a fresh new dozen on her desk.

She turned to look at Jack, "Thank you! For some reason I'm picturing shelves full of withered red roses," she teased.

"I believe that if your day starts off good, it'll continue. The trick is getting it to start off good, and I hope yours did."

"It most definitely did," she said with a kiss. "Thank you for caring so much about my first day."

"Yes, ma'am," he nodded. "Remember, I'm right down the hall or just a phone call away," he reminded her.

"Okay, I'm sure I'll be calling you. Don't worry, Daddy," she said as she started walking Jack toward the door.

"Who's your Daddy?" devilishly grinned Jack.

Once she had said bye to Jack, she sat down to read the list of clients that she was to see. There was a total of six spread throughout the day.

"Staci Webber, hmm! That sounds familiar," she whispered to herself.

Her first client, Staci Webber, was scheduled for 9:30.

On the corner of her desk were the files of all the clients she would see that day.

She picked the phone up and called Isabella.

"Hello," answered Isabella.

"Good morning, Isabella! How are you?"

"Great! How is your first official day going?"

"That's why I called you. Are you the one that was so kind as to bring all these files to my office?"

"Why, yes, I am."

"Thank you so very much! I didn't even know inmates had files," she laughed.

"That's okay. You know I've got your back," she laughed with Mary Jane.

"I have a question for you already," stated Mary Jane.

"Shoot," replied Isabella.

"Well, I was looking through the names of today's clients, and I ran across one that sounds familiar, but I can't place it."

"Say no more. I already know who it is. Staci Webber, right?"

"I knew it. She's been in the news, hasn't she?"

"Oh yeah, she's been in the news. I'm pretty sure she's made the world news a couple of times. Let me give you a hint. She was nicknamed after a famous sculpture in Oregon near Crater Lake, *The Lady in the Woods*. Sound familiar?"

"A little, but I still can't place her. Give me more info."

"Her nickname became the 'Stone Coldhearted Lady in the Woods.' They've even made up ghost stories about her, and people go there to see if they see the ghosts of her family that she murdered. She killed her ten-year-old son, seven-year-old daughter, and her husband. Then she turned herself in three years later after living for those three years in the woods right next to where she buried them."

"Yeah, I do remember the lady that killed her entire family. But wasn't there something else weird about her. Isn't she psycho or something?"

Laughing, Isabella responded, "Of course she is. No sane person would kill their whole family."

"I know that, but wasn't there something else about her case regarding insanity?" asked Mary Jane.

"Oh, yeah. That's right! She refused the insanity plea," remembered Isabella.

"Now I remember. She not only refused the insanity plea but actually requested the death penalty. I remember being so perplexed over that because it was like she did this insane act, but had enough sense to determine what her punishment should be."

"If that perplexes you, get a load of this. The whole time she's been here on death row, she's been taking classes."

"What do you mean classes?"

"I mean bona fide classes. Science classes, I think," answered Isabella.

"What? Why is she taking classes if she's going to be put to death?"

"No one knows. Maybe you can find out when you talk to her."

"Oh, great! Really! On my first day, this is what I get?" Mary Jane laughed.

Teasing, Isabella said, "We figured if you can handle her, you can handle the rest of them with no problem."

"Great! Then I guess I better get to work and show you what I've got. I have one hour to review her chart, so I better let you go and get busy."

"I have to warn you. There are pictures in her file that are very graphic," said Isabella.

"Oh, okay, I'll call you back later. Thanks, Isabella!"

"You're welcome! Talk to you later."

Glancing at the clock, she whispered to herself, "You have thirty minutes to learn as much as you can about this crazy lady."

As she opened the file, the pictures Isabella spoke of were right on top and face up. As Mary Jane looked through them, they seemed to her, to be in the order of the investigation. The first several photos were taken outside of a picturesque home. Large Willow trees hovered over the natural stone house which sat on a gently sloping hill. The beautifully landscaped lawn gave witness to a diligent gardener.

Purple lavender lined the sidewalk leading to the front door, and a variety of brightly colored flowers encircled each tree.

In sharp contrast, the next set of photos were of the interior. Trails of red clumps stained the beige colored carpet in the bedrooms and the hallway. *Slaughter*, thought Mary Jane when she saw the blood-stained beds and pillows. From the pictures of the hallway carpet, she could see that the victims had lost most of their blood in the bedrooms, as only small trails stained the hallway carpet. Then, she came upon the pictures of what was left of Staci Webber's family. After three years in the shallow graves, only small amounts of dried tissue was left on their bones. Each of the family members had their arms neatly folded on their chest. Mary Jane had never seen a decomposed body let alone one that was buried in the dirt. She noticed their clothing was free of blood and figured Mrs. Webber must have dressed all three family members before burying them. After Mary Jane became nauseated and could no longer bear to look at the photos, she read Chief Mitchell's report about Mrs. Webber turning herself in after her three years of living in the woods.

What did she do for three years? Mary Jane wondered. Many questions emerged in Mary Jane's mind. She had a dozen or so questions that she intended on asking Mrs. Webber, but remembered something she learned in orientation. She learned that to successfully earn trust from the prisoners; she would first have to gain rapport with them. She knew she should not ask all the questions she wanted to in one session. This was going to take some time, and she didn't know how much time she had left. After all, Mrs. Webber had already been on death row for three years.

As Mary Jane planned out her upcoming conversation with Mrs. Webber, there was a knock at the door.

"Come in," she answered.

The door slowly opened, and an officer's head appeared as he leaned in and asked, "Are you ready for Mrs. Webber?"

A cold chill ran down Mary Jane's spine, and every hair on her neck stood to attention. Sweat beads began to emerge on Mary Jane's forehead as she noticed her heart beating harder and faster.

The officer saw her discomfort and responded, "I'm going to be right here. Don't worry about a thing, Ms. Scarsdale. You can either see her in the interrogation area or right here in your office, whichever makes you more comfortable."

With a forced and nervous smile, Mary Jane answered, "I believe I'd be more comfortable right here. And, I'm as ready as I'm going to get, so go ahead and bring her in."

The officer reported, "Then, I'll be back in about five minutes with her. Do you want her sitting in that chair across from you or standing?"

"I believe I would like her sitting across from me."

"Okay, I'll bring her in cuffed at the wrists and ankles and sit her in this chair. Then I'll stay right here, standing in that corner. And, don't worry about a thing. Believe me; I won't let her get out of line. The warden already told me to take special care of you. I'm Officer Dave, by the way," he said as he extended his hand with a friendly smile.

Reciprocating his handshake, she said, "Mary Jane Scarsdale. Thank you so much for the reassurance! I really do appreciate it."

"Pleased to meet you, ma'am, and it's my pleasure. So, I'll be back in about five minutes," he said as he backed out into the hall.

Quickly shutting the folder and tidying up her desk, Mary Jane waited for the prisoner to enter her office. In that quick five minutes, she tried to figure out how she should introduce herself. Shaking the prisoner's hand was not an option, so she wasn't sure what she should do.

Before she could decide, came the expected knock on the door. Even though she knew the knock was coming, her startle reflex caused her whole body to flinch.

"Come in," she tried to answer in a calm yet professional tone.

Officer Dave led the prisoner to the chair and said to her in a rough voice, "Sit here!" Mary Jane saw that Mrs. Webber was handcuffed with her arms to the back. Her ankles were also cuffed which caused her to scuffle along as she walked. Seeing Mrs. Webber bound in such a way gave Mary Jane much assurance. Mary Jane looked up at the officer as he backed up to the wall, and with a head nod, gestured for Mary Jane to proceed. Mary Jane smiled up at him to show her appreciation. Then, Mary Jane looked at Mrs. Webber's face just in time to see an expression of distaste over their exchange.

Mrs. Webber's overall appearance was not at all what Mary Jane had anticipated. She had long, shiny, dark, black hair, a smooth complexion, and an overall neat appearance. While pondering how Mrs. Webber had kept herself in such good condition in prison, Mary Jane suppressed the thought and said with a friendly smile, "Hi, Mrs. Webber, I'm Ms. Scarsdale. How can I help you today?"

"I know who you are and what your job is. Your job is to fulfill my last request," she stated with a straight face and a flat tone.

Bewildered by her verbal attack, Mary Jane's relaxed demeanor immediately transformed back into intense anxiety.

In Mary Janes's defense, Officer Dave quickly advanced upon Mrs. Webber. Latching on to her handcuffs, he pulled her arms up behind her, lifting her off the chair. "Watch your mouth! You speak with respect to Ms. Scarsdale, or I will escort you immediately back to your cell."

Mary Jane studied Mrs. Webber's face as she was hoisted upward. Pain was visibly obvious, but not a sound came from Mrs. Webber. She had a hard, cold stare. Her eyes were dark and flat as if there were no life in them.

Mary Jane had seen eyes like hers before in a bait house her dad had taken her to when she was a little girl. She remembered her dad telling her to look at the eyes. That's how you could tell how fresh or old the fish was as it lay on the bed of ice. The old fish had flat, dark eyes with no shine to them. The fresher fish still had shiny, bright eyes.

Like the old fish, there was no life in Mrs. Webber's eyes.

Mrs. Walking Dead echoed in Mary Jane's mind. All of a sudden, Mary Jane had an intense desire to get Mrs. Webber out of her office as soon as possible. The large girth of her new desk became immediately apparent and appreciated by Mary Jane. It kept a good distance between her and "Mrs. Walking Dead," which was now Mrs. Webber's new nickname, as far as Mary Jane was concerned.

No longer concerned about etiquette, Mary Jane quit smiling and flatly asked, "What is your request?"

"I want this phone number listed online under microbiologist," she said as she attempted to slide a piece of paper across the table toward Mary Jane.

The officer quickly stepped over and grabbed her arm. "You know the rules. Don't try that again," he growled as he took the paper from her hand and handed it directly to Mary Jane himself.

Mrs. Webber paid him no mind and quickly explained her request, "I want my name and that phone number listed online under microbiologist for eternity."

Bewildered, Mary Jane looked at the piece of paper, and on it was written a strange phone number, "64276246564478." As far as Mary Jane was concerned, the phone number was nothing but gibberish. It had way too many digits to be considered a legitimate phone number.

Perceiving an opportunity to ask questions, Mary Jane inquired, "As I understand it, you've been given the death penalty, right?"

"That's correct. I'm sure you know that. You have my folder right in front of you," she answered looking directly at the folder under Mary Jane's folded hands.

"Then why, may I ask, do you want this number listed?" Mary Jane persisted on.

"You're better off not knowing. Besides, I don't wish to discuss that with you."

"Fine, I'll take care of your request," boldly stated Mary Jane.

"See to it that you do, or we will be speaking again," Mrs. Webber warned as she rose and looked at the officer to escort her back.

As Mrs. Webber walked out, the eerie feeling in the room lingered like a bad odor. Feeling chilled, Mary Jane reached for her sweater on the back of the chair. As she did, she thought she heard someone whisper, "Another realm." Even though she knew there was no one behind her; she couldn't help but turn to look. As she already knew, no one was there. She looked down at the intercom light on her phone which wasn't lit up, therefore not activated. She walked to the door to look in the hall. No one was near her door.

"Hmm, that was strange. I guess I'm hearing things," she whispered to herself and left it at that.

Having no intention of fulfilling the bizarre request, Mary Jane tried to dismiss Staci Webber from her thoughts, but couldn't.

Forcing her focus on the remainder of the day, Mary Jane began thumbing through the files of the other prisoners, hoping they wouldn't be as insane as the first.

Even though they were not death row inmates, they were high security. There was one in prison for rape of a minor, two for manslaughter, and the other three for armed robbery. Mary Jane was relieved that the rest hadn't murdered their entire families. She thought how odd it was that the murderer, the rapist, and the armed robbers weren't, what she considered, the real bad boys. "Perspective," she said out loud.

Their requests were all fairly sane and easy to accomplish. One wanted to make contact with his children, one requested an attorney, and the rest just wanted to change their current duties to kitchen duty. "They must have heard there was a new opening in the kitchen," Mary Jane humorously thought.

Her decision to not fulfill Mrs. Walking Dead's request, nor tell anyone about it, including Jack, weighed heavily on her mind most of the day. She thought about how she didn't want to start her and Jack's relationship off with secrets between them. At the same time, she didn't want to appear stupid by inquiring about something that was obviously bizarre. Before the day ended, she had convinced herself that it wasn't a secret, but something just not worthy of mentioning. As the first day of her new job came to a close, she finally had a moment to call Jack.

"Hi, Jack."

"Hey, Darlin'. I've been worried about you. Haven't heard from you since lunch."

"Well, I've been working my fingers to the bones," she teased.

"Sounds like you need a glass of wine and a good massage."

"Sounds like you wanna get lucky," she laughed.

"Oh, no! You've already learned to decipher me," he laughed.

"Are you inviting me to sleep over?"

"Will you?" he asked.

"I would appreciate it. I really didn't want to drive all the way home."

"I'm glad you mentioned that. I was going to suggest that you stay with me until you find a place or until you just can't stand me anymore."

"That might take a while," she giggled.

"That's fine with me. I told you, I like you a lot," he reminded her.

"Are we talking suitcase full of clothes or clothes in the closet and my toothbrush in your toothbrush holder?" asked Mary Jane.

"We are talking about your clothes in *our* closet and your toothbrush in *our* toothbrush holder," he boldly answered.

"We've only known each other for five weeks. Are you sure you can handle a woman living with you, Jack?" she asked with concern.

"Not just any woman, but you, yes," he honestly answered.

Once they arrived at Jack's house and were at the front door, Jack stopped before unlocking it and said, "I have a few surprises for you, Mary Jane. I know I was presumptuous, and I hope it's not too much, too soon."

He unlocked the door and then handed Mary Jane the key. Earlier, he had made it for her and placed it on a keychain. The keychain had an engraved heart with the words, "Jack N' Mary Jane."

"Oh, Jack, you're the sweetest, most thoughtful guy in the world."

"That's not all," he proudly said as he led her to the bedroom. He took her to a closet and opened the door. It was empty.

"Yours," he said as he grabbed her hand and led her to the nightstand next to the bed and pulled open the empty drawer.

"Yours, also."

He then led her to the bathroom and pointed to a new pink toothbrush in the holder. "Mine?" Mary Jane asked before he could say "yours" again.

"Yes, ma'am. If you need anything else, all you have to do is ask."

Mary Jane was overwhelmed, but glad that Jack felt the same as she did.

They had a romantic night after a glass of wine and a massage as Jack had promised. She stayed with Jack every night, and after a month his home started to feel like their home. They fished, boated and watched movies on the weekends. During the week, they enjoyed dinner and sitting on the couch while telling each other about their day over an occasional glass of wine. They meshed together like neither of them had with anyone else before. Both knew, in their hearts and minds, that they would one day marry.

᠊ᢀᘓᘓ᠊

Before long, two months had passed, and Jack could no longer contain his love for Mary Jane. Secretly, he made a plan and carried it out on a beautiful Saturday morning in the fall. The temperature had lowered from the steamy nineties to the upper seventies. The weather conditions were perfect for being out on the water, so Jack convinced Mary Jane to go "fishing."

The sky was blue, and there wasn't a cloud in the sky as Jack excitedly trailered the boat from their home in Livingston to a boat ramp under the Kemah Bridge. Once Jack had the boat in the water, he piloted it out where there were no other boats around and stopped. He turned to Mary Jane, who was wondering why they had stopped so soon, and said, "Mary Jane, I have a confession to make."

Mary Jane's heart about stopped, thinking he was going to tell her something horrible. All sorts of terrible things ran through her mind. "Was he married? Did he have a venereal disease? Does he have another girlfriend? What?"

"I love you, Mary Jane!"

Oh, my God, why did he have to scare the hell out of me? she thought, but said, "I'm so glad you do, because I love you too, Jack. I've been in love with you since the day we met."

"Well, I loved you before we met. You're the girl of my dreams," he charmingly confessed.

"What a beautiful place you chose to tell me," smiled Mary Jane.

"There is no place nicer than on the water," he agreed.

From there, they went across the bay to a little restaurant, docked the boat at the pier, and had a romantic seaside lunch.

"We're really not going fishing today. I just wanted to tell you I love you in the most romantic place I know," confessed Jack.

"You sly devil," Mary Jane teased.

Ⅎℭ

Another month passed, and Mary Jane couldn't have been happier. She often thought of the morning when she turned thirty-five and decided that she was going to change her life. At the time, she remembered being very frightened and not so sure she was doing the right thing. But now, she knew that she had made the right choice. After all, if she hadn't made it, she would've never met Jack.

One Monday morning, as fall approached, Jack called Mary Jane on her office phone with some news. He informed her that Mrs. Webber's execution date was nearing. In two weeks, he would be in the death chamber to oversee every aspect of it. Mary Jane wondered if she should confide in him about the odd last wish of Mrs. Webber, but still didn't. The guilt of not being honest with Jack continued to weigh heavily on her mind and her heart. And, even though Mrs. Webber's last request was ridiculous, she couldn't help but feel that she had neglected her job responsibilities, as well. She hoped no one would ever find out, especially Jack.

Mary Jane knew nothing about executions. So, that Monday afternoon, Jack answered all of her questions about it over a glass of wine. In the fifteen years that Jack had been the warden at the Huntsville state prison, he had overseen every single execution held there and knew every detail about them. As they sat cozily on the couch, he explained to Mary Jane that inmates are brought from death row to the Walls Unit early in the afternoon of their scheduled execution. They are placed in a holding cell, which is about 30 feet from the door of the execution chamber. There, all the preparations for the execution are completed. After the prisoner is prepared and the time is at hand, the execution team transfers the prisoner to the execution chamber.

The execution chamber is a 9' x 12' room with turquoise painted walls. It's empty except for a gurney and a small pillow. There is a two square inch hole in the wall which connects to the adjacent cell. The adjacent cell is where the executioner carries out the lethal injections. No one sees nor knows who the executioner is on the other side of the wall.

By law, executions are scheduled to begin only after 6 pm in case they are postponed by the court. Many have been canceled or postponed in the last few minutes for different reasons. Several times, it was due to the lack of or clarity of the medications to be administered.

Also, the inmate scheduled for execution no longer gets a special last meal as they did in the past. Jack explained that the victims' families deemed it unfair due to the fact that their murdered loved ones didn't get a last special meal. The families had argued their case before the House and the Senate and eventually succeeded in changing the law.

He went on to explain that the death row inmate can, but is not required, to make a last statement. Many of the last statements become famous. Jack knew some of those famous last statements by heart and shared them with Mary Jane. "Give my love to my family and friends," were Ted Bundy's last words. In contrast, John Wayne Gacy's final farewell was, "Kiss my ass." The most famous goodbyes, and the ones Jack got the biggest kick out of, actually employ humor. One of his favorites was spoken by James French. Laying on the gurney, about to die, James French smiled and said, "How's this for a headline? 'French Fries.'"

Mary Jane also learned that there are two adjacent observation rooms that overlook the death chamber. One room is reserved for the family of the victim, and the other is for the family of the condemned. As Jack continued sharing his knowledge, Mary Jane wondered if only one observation room would be occupied during Staci Webber's execution. After all, she murdered all of her family members. There was no one, as far as Mary Jane knew, to sit in the room dedicated to the condemned.

Interrupting her thoughts, Jack went on to explain that death usually occurs quickly, within minutes of the order to execute. Unless, of course, something goes wrong. And, there have been cases where things did go awry. Apparently, in some past executions, something had been wrong with the drugs or the way they were administered, because the prisoner did not die right away as planned. They lingered on, gasping for air for half an hour or so. Of course, their suffering was considered inhumane. So every effort is made to see to it that everything goes according to plan, and they expire peacefully and quickly. If there was only one execution drug, there would be less of a chance for error. But there are a total of three drugs that are administered. The first is an anesthetic, sodium thiopental, which puts the prisoner into a deep sleep. He told her that it's the same one used to perform surgeries but in a much higher dose. After about thirty seconds, pancuronium bromide, a muscle relaxant is injected. It's given in a dose that stops breathing by paralyzing the diaphragm and lungs. Then, the toxic agent, potassium chloride, is given as a lethal dose to interrupt heart function which induces cardiac arrest.

"I believe in justice, but those drugs sound awful. I wouldn't want them injected into me," Mary Jane confessed.

"It's actually quite peaceful, especially compared to the old ways when they used 'Old Sparky,'" explained Jack.

"Old Sparky?" Mary Jane inquired.

"Old Sparky was an electric chair which electrocuted the condemned to death. Electrocution was abandoned after being deemed by the Supreme Court as cruel and unusual punishment. Good thing they don't leave it to me. We'd still be hanging them from the tree and leaving them to rot," growled Jack with a teasing smile.

Mary Jane didn't sleep peacefully after learning about execution. She thought it was an ugly business but believed it was a necessary evil.

Chapter 10
Midnight in Texas

*T*wo weeks came and went, and the scheduled day of execution arrived.

Mary Jane, a sketch artist, and three news reporters were allowed to sit in the vacant observation room reserved for Mrs. Webber's family. Usually, a priest would also be present, but Staci Webber refused one.

In the adjacent room, reserved for the victims' family, sat Sam Webber's parents and grandparents, quietly weeping and comforting one another. For seven long years, they had eagerly waited to see justice for their son and grandchildren.

In the dimly lit room, they silently sat in the plastic chairs watching through the big glass window that spanned nearly the whole wall. Soon, the thin glass window would be the only barrier between them and the killer of their beloved offspring.

Just as every execution before, the prisoner was prepared in a room down the hall. The seasoned staff made no attempt to comfort Mrs. Webber as they silently and without regard to modesty, removed her prison attire and placed her in a white medical gown.

"Get up on the gurney and lie flat on your back," instructed the guard. Without a word or a moment's hesitation, Mrs. Webber climbed onto the gurney and voluntarily placed her arms on the outspread arm boards. Within a couple of minutes, the team had her fastened down tight. Black straps were placed, and the buckles tightened around her chest, waist, and thighs. Velcro straps were tightened around her ankles and wrists, holding her firmly to the cold steel table. Then the nurse, who had been waiting against the back wall, stepped forward to complete her share of the preparation. First, she placed incontinent briefs on Mrs. Webber. Then, fast as clockwork, she stuck the intravenous needle in the bend of Mrs. Webber's arm, screwed in the cannula, and attached the tubing. The nurse walked to the other side of the gurney and did the same to the other arm. Mrs. Webber looked up to see what was dripping into her veins. A small smile swept across Staci Webber's face as she remembered the last time she saw saline dripping into her intravenous line. It seemed like only yesterday that she was giving birth to her sweet daughter, Elizabeth.

Jack observed her smile and couldn't contemplate how she could have any emotion other than fear in her last moments. Her smile disgusted him, and he intended to distinguish it.

"Are we fully prepared to transfer the prisoner to the death chamber?" Jack's booming voice echoed through the small room. Her smile disappeared. But to his dismay, he didn't engage a startle reflex in her, but he did in the nurse adjusting the flow of the intravenous fluids. The nurse instinctually turned and frowned at Jack. Silently, he lipped, "Sorry," back to her. She just shook her head as she walked back to the wall.

Jack had seen many hardened criminals break down once they reached the preparation room. It was as though, until that very moment, they continued to believe that they had gotten away with their hideous acts. That was why Jack highly rated the thunderous sound transmission in that room. It seemed to get the attention of the condemned, and it made him feel as if he were one of God's soldiers roaring out the order for their ultimate and justified punishment.

Jack removed the final checklist from his pocket. While glancing back and forth between the paper in his hand and Staci Webber's facial expression, he read it aloud for all to hear. He hoped to see some sort of reaction from Staci Webber. He had no sympathy for her, and secretly he wanted to witness her comprehend her tragic grand finale. For the whole time she was on death row, he had never once seen her exhibit sorrow for her evil acts, nor fear for her own mortality. Unfortunately, she remained stoic throughout the preparation. Maybe, Jack thought, she will break in the execution chamber. After the checklist was validated by all present, they began to file out into the hallway.

At 5:59 PM, and without warning, all witnessing from the observation rooms saw the grey steel door quickly swing open into the execution chamber. First, the observers saw the warden, Jack, enter. Behind him, came a physician in a long white lab coat, a nurse, and three security personnel. Then, Staci Webber was rolled in on the gurney by the last two uniformed officers. Her face yielded no sign of emotion whatsoever—no fear, no regret, no sorrow.

All in attendance wondered if she would make a last statement. If so, what would she say? Would she ask for forgiveness? Would she apologize to her husband's family? Or, would she advertise her demonic religion?

Everyone in the execution chamber jockeyed for their assigned position, and once they were all in place, Jack, who was standing behind Staci Webber at the head of the gurney, asked the anticipated question, "Do you have any last words you would like to state now?"

Uncomfortable silence infiltrated the cell as everyone breathlessly waited for her to speak. Then, the stillness was broken as Mrs. Webber torturously tilted her head back towards Jack. As her eyes met his, she calmly stated, "Today my life begins in another realm. And soon, very soon, the seal will be broken and my master, Abbadon, will be released from the chain that has bound him for 1000 years. He will gather us from the four corners of the earth. Our number is great—as the sands of the sea. Then, the great day of destruction shall be upon you and all that you love. Until that day, we, his angels, are here in multitude and magnitude, gathering every last soul."

Fighting the instinct to step back and away from her eerie posture, Jack stubbornly stood firm. Her words did not penetrate him—he refused them.

Mrs. Webber's last words were not what Sam's parents or grandparents had hoped to hear. Nor, were they what Mary Jane had wished for. An apology for her hellish deeds was desired by nearly everyone attending—that is, besides the news reporters. They yearned for words that were so vile and despicable that they would make even them shudder—words that would give them instant fame and notoriety for reporting them. Disappointed by Mrs. Webber's profitless statement, one news reporter shrugged and whispered to himself, "She's nothing but a crazy bitch."

Shocked, Mary Jane turned to see what kind of man would utter such hideous words at such an event. As her eyes focused on him, his facial expression changed instantly as he appeared to melt in his chair.

"Oh, God, can she hear us from in here?" he turned toward Mary Jane and asked. Puzzled, Mary Jane quickly redirected her eyes back to Mrs. Webber.

Mrs. Webber was glaring directly at the reporter as if she did, indeed, hear the reporter's words.

Mary Jane whispered, "Not that I'm aware of."

Mrs. Webber's eyes stayed fixed on the reporter as Jack instructed the executioner, concealed on the other side of the wall, to prepare for the administration of the drugs.

It was at that exact moment, it dawned on Mary Jane that she had heard Mrs. Webber's words before, but where? She remembered it was the morning that Mrs. Webber was escorted into her office to make a final request. After she made the odd request, and the officer escorted her out of Mary Jane's office, Mary Jane thought she had heard someone whisper, "another realm." At that time, Mary Jane concluded it was just her imagination. But now, she wasn't so sure. Mary Jane studied Mrs. Webber's face hoping to get some sort of answer. It seemed, to Mary Jane, that the words had somehow echoed through time. Of course, no answer was revealed to Mary Jane, and the execution continued. Mary Jane tried, with all her might, to focus on the present. She redirected her thoughts on what Jack had told her about the executioner. Mary Jane forced herself to concentrate on the executioner behind the wall, wondering if she knew him. Jack had explained to her that the executioner stays concealed behind the wall in case the family or friends of the executed decide to seek revenge.

All of a sudden, Mary Jane heard Jack say, "Administer the first round." On the other side of the one-way glass window, the concealed executioner injected the first drug into the tubing that traveled through the small square hole in the brick wall and into Mrs. Webber's arm. In less than a minute, Mrs. Webber's eyes closed. That's when Jack ordered the executioner to inject the second drug. Mary Jane estimated that, once the second drug was injected into the tubing, Mrs. Webber's chest stopped rising and falling within thirty seconds. Jack noted the absence of breath. He motioned for the physician to examine her. The physician placed the stethoscope to the side of Mrs. Webber's chest and listened for a moment. Once the physician was sure that Mrs. Webber's breathing had ceased, he looked at Jack and nodded for him to continue.

"Inject the final drug," Jack ordered. In exactly one minute from the time Jack gave the final order, the physician placed his stethoscope to Mrs. Webber's chest, looked at the clock, and pronounced her dead at 6:17 PM.

Even though Jack had explained to Mary Jane that executions were usually quick and painless for the prisoner, she was astonished after witnessing one for herself. She wondered how families must feel when they see the killer of their loved ones being punished with a drug that seemed to simply induce sleep.

Mary Jane tried to convince herself that it would be acceptable to offer condolences to the Webber family in the other observation room. Deep down inside, she knew her real desire was to hear their thoughts on Staci Webber's punishment. For one minute, she had herself convinced that the proper thing to do was visit them. Then the next minute, she knew it was an invasion of privacy. Back and forth, she argued with herself. In the end, she couldn't go through with it.

Mary Jane's distaste for Mrs. Webber increased tremendously after witnessing her peaceful finish. The way Mary Jane perceived the situation, Mrs. Webber should have suffered a horrendous death for all the pain she had caused.

Twenty minutes after the execution was completed, Mary Jane heard sirens outside the prison walls. The next day, she learned that one of the news reporters was killed in an auto accident as he was pulling out onto the highway. Apparently, he was hit head-on by a drunk driver. Both drivers were pronounced dead at the scene. Luckily, there were no passengers in either car.

Two weeks elapsed and Staci Webber had become a bitter memory for Mary Jane. She was having a difficult time forgetting the ordeal.

One night, as Mary Jane lay in bed trying to fall asleep, Staci Webber's final words echoed in her mind once more. During the execution, Mary Jane thought she had read Staci Webber's words from somewhere in the Bible, but couldn't remember for sure. While she lay there, she suddenly remembered where she had seen Staci Webber's final words. They were from the book of Revelations. Retrieving her Bible, she flipped it open to Revelations and searched till she found it in Chapter 20. When Staci Webber threatened that the 1000 year imprisonment of Satan was near the end, Mary Jane, nor no one else, understood the implications. After Mary Jane read, she hoped that the end of the 1000 years was still a long way off. For, as she understood it, evil was going to be allowed to wreak havoc on the world as never before. She read that Satan was going to be released and would arrive on earth as a beautiful creature. Everyone will be deceived into believing he is God. At first, he will create peace on earth. Then all hell will break loose. Mary Jane didn't believe Staci Webber had any knowledge of when all the foretold events would unfold. She knew Staci Webber was just crazy. But Mary Jane did think it very sad that someone taught Staci Webber what the Bible said. And instead of following righteousness, as the Bible teaches, she chose evil instead.

ॐ ♋

Shortly after, a sunny weekend arrived, and Mary Jane decided to drive to Alvin to catch up with errands and visit her parents. Although she left work early, she still didn't reach her apartment in Alvin until after 8:00 PM.

With the television on for company and a cozy fireplace ablaze, Mary Jane sat on the couch with a load of laundry to fold.

As she was entranced in the peaceful serenity, the phone rang, causing her to jump. She looked at the clock to see what time it was. It was 9:00 PM. Expecting the caller to be Jack, she answered in a sexy whisper, "Hello, Lover Boy."

"Hi, Darlin'," said Jack.

Before Mary Jane knew it, two hours had passed while they conversed. Good nights were wished, and Mary Jane got undressed for bed. She had missed her comfortable bed and snuggled in for a good night's rest. She fell into a deep sleep very quickly.

At the stroke of midnight, the phone rang again. Alarmed and sitting straight up in bed, Mary Jane tried to figure out what the obtrusive noise was that awoke her. By the third ring, she finally figured out it was the phone on her bedside table. She looked at the clock and became immediately alarmed thinking that something must be terribly wrong for someone to call at midnight.

"Hello," she nervously answered.

"You did not fulfill my last request," responded the unknown caller.

Puzzled at the statement and not recognizing the voice on the other end, Mary Jane asked, "Who is this?"

"You already forgot all about me, didn't you?" said the mysterious voice.

"Who is this?" Mary Jane asked with more persistence in her tone.

"Staci Webber," the voice answered.

Cold chills ran up and down Mary Jane's spine as the temperature of the room seemed to drop. Feeling chilled, Mary Jane pulled the bedspread up to her neck. Then, bravely, she stated, "Staci Webber is dead. This is the last time I'm going to ask. Who is this?"

"I told you, Staci Webber."

Mary Jane hung the phone up and tried to figure out why and who would play a prank of that magnitude on her. Her phone number was unlisted, and only Jack and her family knew it. Not even Isabella had her home phone number. The one and only fact she could deduce for sure about the mysterious caller was that the voice was that of a female. Was someone trying to scare her? If so, why? If they had her unlisted phone number, did they also know where she lived? Climbing out of bed to make sure all of the windows and doors were locked, Mary Jane quietly made her way around the dark apartment with the flashlight she kept at her bedside table. Looking through the front window, she saw nothing moving about in the darkness. The neighborhood dogs were quiet. And since they were always the first to sound the alarm at the slightest movement, she knew no one was stalking the perimeter. She wanted to call Jack, but she didn't want to wake him unnecessarily. So, she quickly reconsidered and decided to be brave instead. She made one more round checking the locks on the windows and doors. Knowing she was safely locked in, she went to the bathroom medicine cabinet and took out a sleeping pill. She knew there was no chance of falling back to sleep without one. Returning to bed, she flipped on the bedroom television and waited for the sleeping pill to take effect. Within an hour, she fell back into a deep sleep. Once again, the phone broke the peaceful silence of the night. Only this time, Mary Jane slept right through ring after ring.

When she awoke in the morning, she felt rested after the deep sleep and was no longer worried about the prank phone call. It was a beautiful, sunny day, and she went to visit her parents. She told them all about her new job, her beautiful new office, and about her recent fishing trips with Jack. After they sat on the back porch swing and visited for a while, they decided to plant some seeds in the vegetable garden. Her dad tilled the dirt up with his tractor while she and her mom sowed the seeds.

Exhausted after her busy and fulfilling day, she was ready to get back to her little apartment, shower, and settle in for a relaxing evening of sitting on the couch and watching television. After her nightly conversation with Jack, she laid down for a good night's sleep around 9 p.m. Since she planned to go back to Jack's the next day, she wanted to get as much rest as possible. She contemplated taking a sleeping pill but didn't. Being so tired from working in the garden, she quickly fell asleep.

As she slept peacefully through the dark, moonless night, the silence was broken, once again, by the shrill ringing of the bedside phone. Alarmed, she sat straight up in bed as her heart raced. She looked at the clock, even though she intuitively knew that it would display midnight. Deciding not to answer, she counted fifteen rings, and finally, the phone fell silent. As she sat in bed disturbed and confused, she tried to tell herself it was probably an inmate playing a joke on her. She had heard that prisoners sometimes get insiders to help them for whatever reason. Maybe someone that works at the prison sells phone numbers to prisoners for extra cash. She hashed over numerous scenarios in her mind. As she sat there, the phone screamed out again making her whole body flinch. This time, it made her angry that someone would relentlessly continue to toy with her. So, angrily, she picked up the phone and yelled into it, "I don't know who this is, but I will find out, and you will pay."

Viciously, the female voice responded, "My phone number was not listed. You did not fulfill my last request, and if you don't, you will be the one to pay."

Trying to keep a cool head, Mary Jane tried to think of everyone that knew about Mrs. Webber's strange request. She knew that only Mrs. Webber and the officer that brought her in knew of it. Since Mrs. Webber was dead, that left only the officer. But Mary Jane remembered that the officer didn't see the number.

Now that she realized this, she cleverly decided to call her hand.

"If this is Mrs. Webber, what was the phone number you gave me?"

Sharply, she responded, "I see you are doubting me. Remember, I warned you in our meeting that we would be talking again if you didn't take care of my request. I am very displeased that you did not do what you said you would do. You figure the phone number out. Spell out microbiologist and apply the phone number to it. I know of only one way to convince you. Your beloved Jack will suffer from all of the mercury he consumes from eating fish. He will begin having headaches, and that's when you'll know that his brain tumor is growing."

Mary Jane's redheaded temper flared as the stranger hit a tender nerve. She jumped up and yelled into the phone, "You bitch! How dare you. You just went too far. If I ever find out who you are, I will rip you limb from limb!"

"You are the one to blame. You did not do what you promised. When you do, I will take care of the tumor," the unknown assailant lashed back, and the phone went dead.

As Mary Jane paced back and forth in her bedroom, she could feel her knees shaking and her heart pounding out of her chest. She took deep breaths trying to calm herself. She couldn't recall, in her entire life, ever being so angry. As she paced back and forth, she realized that she needed to calm herself. She was concerned that her blood pressure would be through the roof. Remembering the prescription of Xanax in her medicine cabinet, she immediately went into her bathroom and took one. Then, still trembling, she sat on the couch and tried to recall voices of people she had previously spoken to. She tried to remember what Mrs. Webber's voice sounded like, but she had only talked to her one time and couldn't remember. Besides, there was no way it could have been her. After all, she witnessed Mrs. Webber's death.

After the Xanax took effect, Mary Jane wearily drifted off to sleep. She awoke early Sunday morning to one of the most lucid nightmares she had ever had.

She remembered every detail of the dream—as if it really happened. She found herself wandering barefoot through a graveyard in the same long, white cotton gown that she went to bed in. The moon was bright and full. It cast its glow on the headstones allowing her to read the names inscribed on them. As she passed each gravestone, she read its inscription out loud, "Henrietta Langly, 1929 - 1984, Jason Sanders, 1945 - 2008, Jackie Homer, 1972 - 2011, Ronnie Williams 1924 - 1986." Why am I reading headstones?" she heard herself ask. When at last, she came upon a familiar name. "Staci Webber 1975 - 2018. I knew she was dead," Mary Jane heard herself say. Suddenly, from behind, she heard a woman's voice eerily echoing through the cemetery, "I live in another realm." Mary Jane recalled that the voice was the same one from the midnight phone calls.

Spinning around quickly to see who was there, Mary Jane found herself face to face with Staci Webber who was still dressed in the same prison gown she was executed and buried in. Paralyzed with fear, Mary Jane frantically tried to back away but fell backward onto the ground, never taking her sight off of Staci Webber's cold, dead eyes. Once she struggled her way back up, Mary Jane began running and searching for a way out of the cemetery. All of a sudden, hundreds of people appeared. They were scattered all throughout the cemetery, chanting, "We live in another realm! We live in another realm! We live in another realm!" over and over again. They were not chasing Mary Jane, just standing perfectly still, chanting.

That's when she awoke terrified, sweating profusely with her heart racing as if she had just run a marathon. Her eyes darted around the room looking for Staci Webber. After she realized that she was alone and safe in her bedroom, her heart slowly began to return to a normal pace.

"Am I going crazy? Or is it those crazy phone calls? I need to get a grip on myself," she said out loud.

The next day, she packed and began the long drive back to Huntsville. While driving, she contemplated telling Jack about her nightmare. But she feared that telling him would only lead to more explanation. How she wished she could go back in time and tell him about Mrs. Webber's strange request. Not telling him, was eating her up inside. She felt so dishonest. But overriding that emotion was another. She was also worried that if she did confide in Jack, he would be disappointed in her as an employee. After all, he was not only her boyfriend but also her boss. The way she figured it, in telling him now, she would be upsetting the boyfriend and the boss.

When Mary Jane arrived at Jack's house, he had already made dinner for the two of them and had a bottle of wine chilling in the refrigerator. He looked fine and seemed to feel great, which gave Mary Jane much relief. So, she quickly decided to try and erase the whole Mrs. Webber incident from her mind? They had a lovely afternoon together. Jack's meal was delicious, and the wine relaxed Mary Jane—so much, in fact, she completely forgot about the nightmare and the strange phone calls. After the hearty meal, Jack and Mary Jane snuggled on the couch and watched the evening news together.

On Monday morning, Jack and Mary Jane, no longer trying to conceal their relationship, rode together to work. Upon their arrival, no one said a thing to them, nor reacted as if they were surprised by their attachment. During lunch break, Jack and Mary Jane laughed about the fact that everyone probably figured them out in the beginning, and that they hadn't been as clever as they had thought.

The following weekend, Mary Jane decided she would stay with Jack. She didn't want to face the possibility of getting eerie phone calls at midnight again. They had a lovely weekend together. On Saturday, they went to the casino and met up with some friends of Jack's. Monty and Carol had known Jack for nearly twenty years. They were pleasantly surprised, but at the same time ecstatic, that Jack had finally seemed to find someone he was willing to commit to.

As the two couples played at a card table together, they told Mary Jane all sorts of funny stories about Jack. They laughed heartily all day at Jack's expense. Being comfortable in his own skin, he didn't seem to mind and laughed along with them. Jack and Mary Jane stayed in their complimentary room Saturday night and drove home on Sunday.

Like the week before, they rode to work together Monday morning. When lunchtime rolled around, Mary Jane called Jack.

"Hey, Handsome, would you like to join me for lunch?" she flirted.

"I would love to. Do you have any Tylenol? I have a killer headache," he complained. Fear gripped Mary Jane's very soul, but she tried to hide it. Maybe it was *just* a headache.

"Yes, I actually have some in my purse," she answered unwaveringly.

The moment she laid eyes on his torturous facial expression, she feared it was, indeed, more than just a headache.

"I can see your headache, you poor baby," she said as she ran her hand over his forehead.

"Ahh, that cold hand feels great!"

"When did it start?" she asked.

"Yesterday, on the way home. But it was barely noticeable. It's been getting worse and worse throughout the day," he explained.

Jack took the Tylenol, and Mary Jane silently watched him during the hour they were together for lunch. At the end of the hour, she saw no improvement in Jack's painful expression.

"Jack, do you want me to drive you home? I don't think you should stay the rest of the day."

"Oh, no. I'm sure the Tylenol will kick in soon."

"Well, I have an appointment with a client in about ten minutes. So, I'll check on you as soon as I'm done," Mary Jane said reassuringly.

"Don't worry! It's just a headache. I'll be fine. Take care of business."

Unconvinced, Mary Jane walked Jack back to his office and continued on to hers. The meeting with the prisoner lasted about thirty minutes. The prisoner, glad to be out of his cell, squandered the time away. His only request was a visit from his children. Mary Jane figured that the meeting should have taken ten minutes at the most. As soon as the prisoner was escorted out of her office, she called Jack to see how he was doing.

"I think you might have to drive home today. My head is really hurting."

"Is it bad enough to go to the doctor?" she asked.

"Oh, no! I have to be practically dying to go to the doctor."

Not the words I want to hear, she thought. "Okay, but call me if it gets too bad to handle."

"Will do. We only have one more hour to go anyway."

A few minutes before quitting time, Mary Jane walked to Jack's office. When she walked in, Jack was resting his head on the desk but looked up when she walked in. As he looked up, she saw his face. It was all red and wrinkled from him squashing it against his forearm.

"Jack, you look terrible."

"I really do feel awful. I hate to admit it, but I may need to go to the emergency room. I'm sure there's no doctor still open. It hurts so bad; I feel like I might pass out."

She held on to him all the way to the truck. Even though he was in excruciating pain, he chuckled a little and said, "You're just a little girl! Please don't let me fall on you and squash you like a bug."

By that time, Mary Jane was so worried for Jack; she couldn't laugh with him. They both remained quiet until they reached the truck. She helped him into the passenger seat and buckled him in. Every morning on their way to work, she had seen a hospital and knew exactly where it was.

Chapter 11
Convinced

Luckily, there were only a few patients in the emergency room. As soon as Mary Jane filled out the admitting papers, a nurse walked them to an examining room. The nurse quickly hooked Jack up to monitors and obtained his vital signs. Soon after, a doctor arrived at Jack's side.

"What brings you in to see us today," the doctor asked while looking down at Jack. Mary Jane became instantly irritated since she had written the answer to that question on nearly every piece of paper that she had filled out. She had also already explained the reason for their visit to the nurse. Before Jack had a chance to answer the doctor, Mary Jane snapped.

"How many times do we have to tell y'all? This is Jack Wilson, the warden of the prison. He is one tough hombre. He hasn't seen a doctor since he came out of his mother's womb. But today, he's having a killer headache and needs something for pain, like right now. Did you not look at his chart?"

Without showing any emotions from the assault, the doctor called out for the nurse, "Catherine, please come start an I.V. on Mr. Wilson and draw a CBC, please." He then extended his hand to Mary Jane and said, "I'm Doctor Mathews. I understand you're concerned for Mr. Wilson, but from my twenty-five years of experience as an emergency room physician, I know the value of keeping a good working relationship between me and my patients and their families. So, let me explain, while Catherine is starting an I.V. on Mr. Wilson, why I don't know your story yet. You see ma'am, I've been busy in the next room with an eleven-year-old with a ruptured appendix. He's being admitted right now and is on his way to surgery. I came directly in here from next door because I wanted to get in here as soon as possible. I was told that Mr. Wilson was in a great amount of pain. If I would have stopped to read his paperwork, I would still be out there. I wanted to come in here first because that is the fastest way for me to help him."

Mary Jane was embarrassed that she had acted the way that she did but didn't know what to say right at that moment. So, she remained silent as the nurse called out, "The I.V's in and the CBC is drawn, Dr. Mathews."

"Are you allergic to any medication, Mr. Wilson?" the doctor asked.

"Not that I'm aware of," he answered

"Have you ever had morphine?"

"I don't think so," answered Jack.

"We are going to give you some right now. Let me know if you experience any unpleasant side effects," explained Dr. Mathews.

"Administer 2mg of Morphine please," he ordered to the nurse.

"Yes, sir," Catherine answered as she reached into her pocket and pulled out a tiny glass vial. Mary Jane watched as she inserted a needle into the vial and withdrew the contents.

"Excuse me as I step out to look over his chart. As soon as I get the results of the CBC, which should be very soon, we'll run a CT scan also. For now, the morphine should give him relief," said Dr. Mathews.

"This should make you feel much better within moments," Catherine said to Jack as she emptied the syringe into his I.V.

"He will probably sleep for a while as the doctor looks over his paperwork," Catherine said as she looked at Mary Jane. Mary Jane couldn't decide if that was just helpful information or was intended as a backlash. No sooner than the nurse walked out of the room, Jack smiled up at Mary Jane, who was once again by his side and said, "Hey, Tiger. That's your new nickname. I'm gonna marry you one day."

Rubbing Jack's forehead, Mary Jane smiled down at Jack and said, "I would be very proud to call you my husband. And, I'm so sorry if I embarrassed you."

"You can't do anything to embarrass me," slurred Jack as he drifted off to sleep.

Mary Jane leaned over and kissed Jack on his relaxed forehead. She no longer saw pain in his face as she sat by his side and watched him sleep.

After about thirty minutes, a nurse came into the room and explained to Mary Jane that she was taking Jack to radiology. Mary Jane felt helpless as the nurse rolled Jack's gurney out of the room. Soon, a different nurse came in and asked Mary Jane to wait in the waiting area. As she sat alone in the now crowded waiting room, she grieved for Jack. Quietly weeping, she wished she could go back in time and post the phone number. Then, she remembered what the voice on the phone said about spelling out the word microbiologist. So, she quickly retrieved a pen and paper from her purse. Employing her cell phone, she transposed the spelling of microbiologist into the phone number. Once she saw the numbers—64276246564478—on paper, she stared at them in horror and was barely able to redirect her attention as she heard the nurses wheeling Jack back into the room. They were the exact same numbers Mrs. Walking Dead had given her. She quickly placed the paper back in her purse for safe keeping.

After Jack was back in bed and the morphine began to wear off, he began moaning in pain again. The nurse came in with another morphine injection. Within a couple of minutes, Jack, again, began to feel relief. Soon after, the emergency room doctor came in and informed them that Jack would have to be admitted for the night for pain control. Throughout the night, as soon as the morphine wore off, Jack elapsed back into excruciating pain. Each time, the nurse gave him another injection. In the morning, a doctor came into Jack's room with a troubled look on face.

"Hi, I'm Dr. Fredrick, the neurologist here at the hospital. I understand you came in last night with a severe headache."

"Yes, the worst headache I've ever had," Jack slurred from the morphine.

"I'm sorry, but I have rather disturbing news for you," the doctor said. "We found the source of your headache on the CAT scan we performed yesterday. I'm sorry to inform you that there is a mass causing your headache. The good news is that it is operable. But the sooner you have surgery, the better. If the headache came on you as suddenly as you say, we don't know how fast it is growing."

Mary Jane dropped her head into her hands and began to sob. The doctor said, "Ma'am, I'm sorry! I know this is tough to hear, but I really believe that with surgery, Mr. Wilson will be fine."

He doesn't know the half of it, thought Mary Jane. This could have all been avoided.

Jack didn't know whether it was the tumor or the news of the tumor, but something exacerbated the pain to a level he couldn't take. He cried out, "Please get the nurse right now. I need pain medicine. Please, hurry!"

Mary Jane ran out of the room and to the nurses' station as fast as she could.

"Please, hurry! Jack needs pain medicine now!" she pleaded in a panic.

A nurse jumped up from the computer where she was charting and quickly retrieved another vial of morphine. Once she injected the morphine, Jack began to drop off to sleep.

"Thank you!" Mary Jane sighed. "Did you give him a larger dose? It seems that he went to sleep faster this time."

Sternly, the nurse gazed at Mary Jane and said, "This could have all been avoided," Without giving Mary Jane time to respond, the nurse quickly turned away and walked out of the room.

"What did you say?" Loudly responded Mary Jane. But it was too late. The nurse was apparently no longer within hearing distance. Mary Jane peered out of the room. The nurse was nowhere to be seen.

All of a sudden, Mary Jane realized that the nurse that had just given Jack pain medicine was not the same nurse that had given him the previous injections. Her attention quickly turned to Jack. She quickly ran to his side and placed her hand on his chest to see if he was still breathing. Beneath her hand, she could feel his chest slowly rise and fall. Immediately, she made her way out to the nurses' station to find that one nurse. Several nurses were sitting at the station charting, but none that resembled the nurse that was just in Jack's room.

"Where is the nurse that just gave Jack pain medicine?" she asked as she walked up to the station.

"Ma'am, I'm Jack's nurse, remember me?" one of them said.

"Yes, I remember you, but you're not the nurse that just gave Jack pain medicine," answered Mary Jane.

"No one else should be giving Jack medicine but me," she answered and turned toward the other nurses. "Who gave my patient in room 1165 pain medicine?"

Each one of them said they hadn't even gone into Jack's room much less injected pain medicine.

"Do any of them look like the one that came into the room?" asked the nurse.

"No. I don't see her," Mary Jane professed.

"Ma'am, we are the only nurses on this unit. If someone gave him pain medication, it had to be one of us," she said, as she sternly looked at Mary Jane with the same cold eyes Staci Webber had.

Frozen in the nurse's glare, Mary Jane began to feel that she and Jack were in grave danger. She wondered how many of "them" there were.

The nurse's words began to repeat over and over in her head. "This could have all been avoided. This could have all been avoided."

Mary Jane decided to retrieve her iPad out of the truck and list the phone number right away. She had nothing to lose.

"I'm going to the truck to get my iPad. I'll be right back," she informed the nurse. The nurse strangely smiled at Mary Jane with an agreeable head nod, as if she knew exactly why she was going.

The phone number was placed under microbiologist, as Jack slept completely oblivious that his life was on the line, possibly because of an unlisted phone number.

For three solid hours, Mary Jane watched over Jack as he slept without moving a single muscle or even twitching an eyelid.

At the end of the three hours, miraculously, Jack opened his eyes and looked at Mary Jane without pain in his face. He asked, "Did I already have surgery?"

Smiling, Mary Jane answered with much relief, "No, do you feel better?"

"I still have a headache, but it's much better," he said confused. "Did they give me something different?"

"Not to my knowledge. You had a morphine injection three hours ago, and you've been sleeping ever since."

"I've lost track of time. What time is it? Better yet, what day is it?" he asked as he yawned.

"It's Tuesday, about noon," she said choking back tears.

"You mean, I've only been here one night?" he asked in confusion.

"Yes, we went to the emergency room yesterday afternoon," she explained, as she stood next to him squeezing his hand.

"I don't know exactly what happened, but I sure am glad you're not in pain anymore. Maybe whatever it was, is gone."

"I sure hope you're right," he said as he began rubbing his head, searching for the pain in disbelief.

When word spread of Jack's improvement, the nurse notified Dr. Fredrick who was not a believer in miracles, but of medicine.

Intrigued by the gossip spreading quickly through the small unit, the doctor paid them another visit.

"Hi Jack, do you remember me?"

"I know a doctor came in and saw me, but I was hurting so bad, I couldn't tell you if you were the same one or not. I'm guessing you are."

"I'm the one. Do you remember that I told you that we found a tumor on the CT scan?"

"Yes, I do remember that."

"I've been told that you're having a reprieve from the pain."

"Oh, is that what this is? Is that normal?" Jack asked with disappointment.

"Not really, but the brain sometimes does mysterious things."

Mary Jane interrupted, "Before we go on with any plans, we would like another scan just to make sure."

Surprised at her assertiveness, Jack looked at her and agreed, "That's not a bad idea, doc. I would like to make sure before you split my melon open."

Shaking his head, he said, "Only if you insist. But I have to warn you that CT scans put out a lot of radiation. They're not something you treat like an x-ray. First, let me show you the image we saw on the scan."

"That's not necessary, Dr. Fredrick. We definitely want to do the scan again," stubbornly repeated Mary Jane. The doctor could see that Mary Jane was not going to take no for an answer.

"Ok, I'll schedule it," said the doctor in an irritated tone.

"Thank you," said Jack as the doctor walked out the door.

"He was displeased," noted Mary Jane.

"And how," grinned Jack. "Thanks for being my angel and

taking such good care of me."

"I can't let anything happen to you yet. You're still in first place in our fishing tournament," teased Mary Jane trying to keep Jack from worrying.

Five hours went by before the nurse came to take Jack for his second CT scan, and another two hours before the doctor came back to the room with the results. The doctor entered the room with a confused look on his face and his laptop in his arms.

His words reflected his demeanor. "I'm going to be honest with you folks. I'm stumped. Let me show you why."

Turning the laptop toward Jack and Mary Jane, he explained, "This first image shows the tumor." He pointed to a large dark area. "See how large this mass is?"

He pushed a few keys on the laptop and said, "Now look at this second image. Right here is where the dark mass was before. On this image it's not there," he said as he circled the area with his finger. He then turned and looked at Jack with a tightly crinkled forehead and asked, "How do you feel?"

"I feel much better. The pain is completely gone now."

"Well, I'm glad you feel better, but there has to be a logical explanation for this. Maybe your first scan was mixed up with someone else's. I'm going to get to the bottom of this and let you know." With those last words, he was gone.

Jack was discharged from the hospital that night. The two of them happily went home but never heard from Dr. Fredrick again. After their exhausting visit to the hospital, Jack and Mary Jane decided not to go to work the next day. Instead, they stayed home and appreciated each other's company all day.

Chapter 12
Be Vigilant

With a new appreciation for life, they loved and laughed the entire Wednesday. They also realized just how much they loved each other.

"Jack, I was so afraid that I was going to lose you," she confessed.

"I was afraid you were, too," he laughed.

"Seriously Jack, yesterday made me realize how much in love with you I really am," she said with tears in her eyes.

He pulled her head into his muscular chest and responded to her honestly. "I know. I feel the same. I want you always. I meant what I said yesterday if you were wondering."

"Exactly which statement are you referring to?" she asked as she pulled her head away from his chest to look into his eyes.

Looking into her eyes, he said, "You're the one. I'll never forget the way you stood by my side and took care of me yesterday when I couldn't take care of myself. I loved you before, but now I have a huge appreciation for your character. You're a good girl, Mary Jane. I know we haven't been together very long, but I know in my heart, we're going to be married one day."

Smiling, she said, "I was wondering if you were going to remember saying that."

"Barely. That morphine made me so dopey, but I had to have it. I've never had pain like that. I'm like the doctor—stumped."

Thinking that the perfect opportunity had arrived to tell him everything about Staci Webber, she declined. She just couldn't. She couldn't stand the thought of telling Jack something so insane. He would surely think she was crazy. Besides, she wasn't convinced herself. It had to be purely coincidental that Jack got better after the phone number was listed. Maybe Jack's CT scan images did get mixed up with someone else's. She realized that she would never know for sure.

They rode to work together for the rest of the week. When the weekend arrived, Mary Jane needed to go home again to pay bills, water plants, and visit with her parents.

On her first night back, after telling Jack goodnight over the phone, she curled up in her comfortable bed for a good night's sleep. As Mary Jane slept soundly, the phone rang and woke her. No longer worried about eerie phone calls, she didn't bother looking at the time but just picked up and sleepily answered, "Hello."

"Hello," the familiar voice responded.

Sitting straight up and looking at the time, she said again but in question, "Hello?"

"Can you hear me?" the voice asked.

"Yes."

"I see that you were able to decipher the spelling of microbiologist with the phone number, and I wanted to thank you for listing it," the voice said.

"Your welcome! Who is this again?" she asked still in disbelief.

"You know this is Staci Webber. I see that you still have doubts, but I really don't understand why. I believe I gave you a sufficient amount of evidence," she stated.

"Yes, but I don't understand. I saw Staci Webber die, yet you expect me to believe that I'm talking to her right now.

"Since you fulfilled my request, I will explain again. At my execution, I said that my life would begin in another realm. That's where I am now. Do you know of Newton's Law of Energy?"

"Yes," Mary Jane answered.

"He was correct. He said that once energy exists, it can't become extinct. It can never disappear. It can, however, be transferred. Our souls are energy. They can never just disappear. They are transferred. I was simply transferred to this present realm. I will always exist because my soul is energy."

"I can understand that, but how is it possible for our phone service to connect to whatever realm you're in?"

"Quite simple, actually. Cellular technology has made that possible. It's easier for me to call you than it is for you to call someone on the other side of the world—China, for instance, would be much more difficult for you to reach."

"But who, here, do you need to call?"

"Abbadon, as well as the rest of his angels, have many godly traits. Unfortunately, being omniscient is not one of them. We need a simple and efficient communication system between the two realms. Simply stated, we need cell phone service to communicate back and forth.

"I think I know your next question, so I'll answer it now. There are many, many of us existing on earth, still very much alive, doing our master's bidding. I have to say; I'm always surprised how ignorant you Christians are. You claim to be a Christian, yet you have no idea what the Bible says. Everything you need to know is there. Yet, you have no idea. You ask me, an angel of the Antichrist. I know full well what it says. If you read Genesis Chapter 6, you will see how we came into being. Also, the book of Enoch gives an excellent description of our existence."

Determined to get all of her questions answered, Mary Jane quickly changed the direction of their conversation.

"I will definitely read that, but I have a couple more questions I was hoping you could answer."

"What else would you like to know?"

"Why did you get a degree in microbiology if you knew you were going to be executed to death?"

"Because that's my role here. I use what I've learned to help with The Great Destruction. We destroy man while their souls are still available," she answered.

"I don't understand. How do you use microbiology for destruction?"

"You have to understand microbiology to understand viruses, bacteria, DNA, chemistry, the human body, and every other lifeform on earth."

"But how do you use it to destroy mankind?"

Staci chuckled at her ignorance and said, "It's very easy. We watch and wait for man to make himself susceptible. For example, in Jack's case, I used the mercury-laden fish he ingests on a regular basis to help form a tumor. Mercury is a neurotoxin, meaning it has the ability to cross the blood-brain barrier and cause damage to brain cells. It can cause depression, Alzheimer's, cancer, and so many other disastrous diseases. Cigarettes make my job very easy, as well. There are millions of pathways that lead to man's destruction. Usually, we watch and wait, but sometimes we must coax a man into doing what he knows he shouldn't. Alcohol works as a good adversary in that case. We use alcohol a great deal. When man drinks alcohol, he'll do almost anything we want him to. We can easily trick him into taking someone's life or even taking his own. Fortunately, man is quite easy to destroy since he is always placing himself in jeopardy one way or the other." Staci took a deep sigh and continued.

"Of course, I'll never know as much as my master. When Abaddon was cast out of Heaven and onto Earth, he freely roamed for five thousand years. Can you imagine how much you can learn in five thousand years? He knows every virus, every bacteria, every form of every disease, how to calculate a man's every move, and every crack and crevice in this earth. He is so intelligent that he even created religions that hate God's people in order to kill and destroy them. Even though he has been bound in the great abyss for 1000 years, he still has control over the earth. I, and all the rest of Abaddon's army, wage war against God's creation every single day. As I warned at my execution, my master will soon be released from the chain that has bound him for 1000 years. The world as you know it will soon change."

Those were her last words as the phone went dead. Mary Jane was covered from head to toe in sweat and goosebumps. She was, at last, convinced that the voice did belong to Staci Webber.

ॐ

Before the sun came up, Mary Jane awoke, fully aware that she was a different creature than the day before. She was scared, paranoid, and self-conscious about every move she made. At first, she didn't even want to get out of bed, in fear that she would somehow make a fatal mistake. Then she realized that staying in bed could also cost her. She could develop a blood clot from staying static too long.

"I'm going to have to make some smart changes. I'm not going to let them get me," she said to herself as she located a pen and paper.

Sitting at the kitchen table, she began to take notes of everything that she normally does on a daily basis. She started at the beginning of the day.

"1. Drink coffee," she wrote and looked at the coffee pot.

"Hmm, is coffee good for you or bad for you?" she questioned. She didn't know, so she retrieved her iPad and began investigating. All of a sudden, panic struck her as she realized Jack was by himself and didn't know the dangers that were lurking all around him.

It was early in the morning, still dark in fact when she started driving. She knew she must be very careful for there were probably demons flying over the top of her car, just waiting for an opportunity to destroy her before she could get home to warn Jack.

Driving in the far right lane, she slowly and carefully steered her car toward her second home in Livingston. All the way, in her rearview mirrors, she watched each vehicle as it approached and eventually passed. She could see in her peripheral vision that one particular car had slowed down and was cruising right next to her. She was afraid to look over at the driver. But she knew that she must, for she sensed that someone was glaring directly at her. So, she forced herself to turn and look at the driver.

"No!" she screamed out in terror as she looked directly in the face of Staci Webber. "It can't be you! You're dead!" Slamming her foot onto the brake pedal, her car fishtailed back and forth all over the highway nearly hitting the car next to her. Somehow, she was able to gain control and pull over onto the shoulder. Sobbing uncontrollably into the palms of her hands, she cried out, "Why are you doing this to me? I advertised your number just like you asked."

"Tap, tap, tap," she heard on her window. Startled, she quickly looked up even though she was terrified that it would be Staci Webber. But to her relief, it was a police officer instead. Confused and not sure she was seeing what was really there, she studied the officer's face.

"Ma'am, can you please roll your window down?" he politely asked.

"Can you please show me your badge?" she cautiously requested.

He placed his badge up to the window and stated, "I'm Officer Jackson with the Livingston Police Department, ma'am. Just crack your window, so we can talk."

"Okay," she answered and rolled her window about halfway down.

"Ma'am, I saw you lose control of your vehicle. Have you had anything to drink this morning?"

"Oh, no, sir," she answered.

"Well, what happened, ma'am? What caused you to lose control?"

Thinking quickly, she knew she couldn't reveal the truth, so she tweaked it just a bit.

"The car next to me swerved into my lane just a little, and I overcorrected trying to avoid a collision."

"Ma'am, I'm going to have to ask you to step out of the car and complete a sobriety test," he stated.

"Yes, sir! But as I told you I haven't been drinking," she said as she opened the door.

On the shoulder of the highway, in the bright spotlight of the patrol car, she successfully completed all of the sobriety tests.

"Ma'am, can you please come sit in the patrol car while I investigate the situation?"

"Are you arresting me?" she nervously asked.

"No, ma'am," he answered.

"I don't understand. I didn't do anything wrong. I just swerved to avoid a wreck," she inquired.

"Ma'am, I have been behind you for quite some time, and you and I have been the only two vehicles on the highway for miles. There was no other vehicle next to you when you swerved," he stated.

"I don't know what to say. There was. Maybe their tail lights were out or something, and you didn't see them."

"Ma'am, do you have any medical condition that might explain this?"

"No! There was a car. I saw it very clearly."

"I'm going to need your driver's license and registration, please," he said.

Perplexed, Mary Jane opened her car door and retrieved her driver's license and registration as asked. After she handed them over to the officer, he gently escorted her to the backseat of his patrol car. As Mary Jane contemplated her confusing circumstances, she listened as the officer radioed her information into the station. And, of course, she had a clean record just as she had stated.

"Ma'am, I could just let you go, but my instincts tell me not to. Do you have anyone that can come pick you up?"

"I suppose," she hesitantly answered.

"I'll wait here until they arrive. Where would they be coming from?"

"Only about ten minutes away."

He escorted her back to her car to retrieve her cell phone.

"Jack, don't be alarmed, but I need a ride," she said trying to sound as if everything were fine.

"Okay, where are you?"

"On 59 just past 190, headed your way," she answered?

"Did you break down?"

"No, I'll explain when you pick me up," she answered.

"Are you okay?" he anxiously asked, as he quickly jumped up out of bed and stumbled while slipping his jeans on.

"I'm fine. Don't worry, please! I'll see you when you get here. Drive safely!" she said and quickly disconnected before he could ask any more questions that she didn't know how to answer.

Jack was surprised to see a patrol car as he approached the location Mary Jane had given him.

He slowly came to a stop behind the patrol car and stepped out.

Officer Jackson stepped out of his patrol car and immediately recognized Jack Wilson as the warden of the prison.

When he saw Jack, he declared to himself that he had done the right thing by listening to his instincts. If he had let her go and something awful had happened, he would have been in serious trouble, especially since she was somehow attached to the warden. Jack swiftly walked toward Officer Jackson.

"Good morning, Warden," greeted Officer Jackson.

"Good Morning! What's going on?" bullishly asked Jack.

"No problem, Warden. Ms. Scarsdale just gave me a bit of a scare, and for her safety, I asked her if someone could give her a ride home," the officer tried to calmly explain.

As Jack eyed Mary Jane in the back of the patrol car, he became offended for her and turned his eyes directly back to Officer Jackson.

"Exactly, how did my Fiancé scare you?" questioned Jack.

Now questioning his decision, Officer Jackson explained, "Let me start from the beginning. I was sitting on 59 with my radar, and I saw a vehicle approaching that was swerving just a bit. So, I thought I would follow it and observe through Livingston. And, as I was following Ms. Scarsdale, she seemed to lose control of her vehicle. She began fishtailing all over the highway. I thought she was going to roll. But luckily, she regained control and pulled off on to the shoulder. I completed a sobriety test, which she passed. I asked her what happened, and she said that there was a vehicle next to her which swerved into her lane. The problem is, there were no other vehicles. She seems to be convinced that there was. That's why I'm concerned for her safety."

"I see," responded Jack. "In that case, thank you! I'll take her now."

Mary Jane quickly climbed out of the back seat when Jack opened the back door of the patrol car.

"Are you okay?" asked Jack.

"I'm not sure," Mary Jane answered with a weak smile. "Let's talk in private, on the way home," she requested.

"Sure," Jack complied as he led her to his truck with his arm draped over her shoulders.

Once inside the truck, Mary Jane became teary-eyed and confided in Jack. "I'm not sure what happened. Maybe I was seeing things. Maybe I wasn't. Maybe the execution of Mrs. Webber has given me post-traumatic stress syndrome or something. I don't know. The officer said that there wasn't another vehicle. Jack, before I say this, I want you to know that I realize what I'm about to say is completely unrealistic. But I swear, it seemed so real. I can't believe that it wasn't."

"Mary Jane, I want you to take a few deep breaths. Just stop talking for one full minute, and then tell me what you saw," Jack said, interrupted her rambling.

"Okay," she said as she tried choking back her tears.

An awkward silence fell upon them for the first time since they met. Mary Jane continued to breathe heavy with anxiety from the event. The more she thought about it, the more anxious she became.

Hearing her breathe and seeing the anxiety in her face, Jack knew he had to help calm her nerves.

"Mary Jane, I want you to breathe with me. We're going to breathe in and out slowly. Okay?" he calmly instructed.

"Okay," she nervously answered.

After several minutes of Jack slowly breathing in and blowing out with Mary Jane following his lead, her heart rate and breathing began to slow. After a couple of minutes, Jack lovingly asked, "Better now?"

"I think so," she responded.

"Okay, slowly, tell me what you saw," Jack said.

Mary Jane took a deep sigh and decided she was going to tell Jack everything. She thought that the guilt of keeping the secrets from Jack was catching up with her—making her crazy.

"Okay. What I think I saw was a car pull up next to me. I looked over, and the driver was looking right at me. And, she looked exactly like Staci Webber. It scared me, and I hit the brakes. The car started going all over the road. I was able to get control, and I pulled over. That's when the officer knocked on my window. He thought I was drinking, but I wasn't. He said there wasn't another car. Maybe he just didn't see it."

Until that moment, Jack thought he could handle any situation, but he didn't even know what to say. Another awkward silence fell upon them.

Finally, he decided it was best, for then, to agree with Mary Jane.

"Maybe he didn't see the other car," Jack said without conviction in his voice. Mary Jane heard the doubt in his words. She knew she was to blame, not Jack.

"That's not all. Jack, I hope you know how much I care for you, but I've kept some things from you that I shouldn't have. I kept them from you because they are utterly crazy. Even though they make no sense, I must tell you everything now," she confessed with another deep sigh.

"I'm listening," Jack eagerly invited her to confess her secrets.

Chapter 13
The Truth Shall Set You Free?

Mary Jane started from the beginning with Staci Webber's strange telephone number request. Then, she told him about the midnight phone calls and the strange dreams. She told him about the reason for his hospital visit and the nurse with the cold dead fish eyes. She told him about the voice she heard whisper, "another realm," in her office. She told him everything in one breath with no break in between. Her last words were, "I'm sorry I kept this from you. It's just that it is all so crazy. It happened to me, and even I have trouble believing it. I don't know what you're going to do with it. I'm afraid that now you're going to think I'm crazy. And, I can't say that I blame you."

Again. Jack was flabbergasted and had no idea what to think or say.

He believed that Mary Jane might have been correct when she mentioned post-traumatic stress disorder. Maybe, he thought, the execution and his recent hospital experience were too much for Mary Jane to handle.

"Mary Jane, I love you! I'm not sure what's going on here, but I want you to know that I'm going to stay by your side just like you stayed by mine. We'll figure it all out together," he reassured.

After hearing his response, she knew that he wasn't capable of believing any of what she had just told him. It appeared to her he thought she was mentally ill.

The next day, her fears were confirmed. It was Saturday morning, and Jack awoke her with a good morning kiss and a fresh cup of coffee.

"Good morning, Beautiful," Jack said with a loving smile.

"Good morning," answered Mary Jane. Hesitantly, she accepted the coffee.

"I love coffee with you on Saturday morning," he said as he climbed into bed next to her.

"Actually, I wanted to talk to you about the coffee," she said.

Frowning in confusion, Jack asked, "What's wrong with the coffee?"

"Here's the thing, Jack. I read about coffee, and it is incredibly bad for you."

"I love you, Mary Jane. But I want my coffee in the morning," he responded with a halfhearted laugh.

"Let me tell you what I read. Then you'll understand. You won't want it then either."

"Sweetie, we can't avoid everything that's bad for us. I gave up coffee once before, and I'm not doing it again. It gave me a terrible headache, and I turned into a bear. You don't want to live with a bear, now do you?" smiled Jack.

"Please just listen before you drink it," she pleaded.

"Okay," he succumbed as he hesitantly placed the full cup of steaming coffee on his lap.

"I read that coffee elevates your blood sugar, which in turn leads to arterial deterioration and increases cardiovascular disease. It elevates stress hormones and triglycerides. It lowers serotonin, which promotes anxiety and reduces sleep. And a whole lot of other bad stuff. So much that I can't remember all of it," she rambled on.

"I don't even understand half of what you just said," he laughed.

"And, the water that we make the coffee with is another thing. I want to use filtered water from now on. I don't want us to drink the water that comes from the tap. Do you know what's in that?"

she asked.

Jack couldn't help but laugh.

"This isn't funny, Jack!" she seriously proclaimed.

"Mary Jane, I'm going to be honest and straightforward with you. Something is screwing with your head. I want you to see our psychiatrist at the prison before you come back to work. Maybe the execution bothered you a lot more than you realize. Or, maybe our trip to the hospital really scared you, and it's affecting you in a negative way."

"Maybe you're right. Maybe I just need a little time."

"Well, just know that I'm here to protect you, and I'll do whatever I can to keep you safe. But we can't avoid everything that can harm us. We can't live in a bubble. That's not living."

"I know you're right," she admitted, but inwardly she intended to make some changes.

As they watched the morning news together, Jack drank coffee, and Mary Jane drank filtered water. Out of the corner of her eye, Mary Jane could see Jack looking over at her from time to time. She could see that he was worried.

Later that day, after Mary Jane finished washing clothes, she decided it was time to go shopping for the week.

She made sure to wear the seatbelt, which she hadn't always done in the past. She came up with a new routine for driving through intersections.

Three times, she looked each way, before crossing through every intersection, even if her light was green. She didn't care that other drivers were honking behind her as she slowed to a virtual stop.

Relieved to have made it to the grocery store, Mary Jane parked as close as she could to the front entrance. She figured that with less distance, less could go wrong. She had already decided that she was going to buy only organic fruits and vegetables. And, the meat would have no hormones and no antibiotics. Not only that, but the meat she and Jack would consume from then on would be lean. That meant no more beef—only chicken and turkey. Fish would have been on her list if it weren't for Jack's previous scare.

With her cart half full of organic fruits and vegetables, she walked toward the meat aisle. As she passed others who were pushing their carts through the store, she began to feel that she was being watched. With each passing, she looked into the strangers' eyes as they strolled by. Some were smiling pleasantly and seemed perfectly harmless, completely ignorant of the evil all around them. But others possessed those cold, dead fish eyes. They seemed to pass in slow motion as their glare entrapped Mary Jane's attention. She knew what they were. They were the descendants of the fallen angels that Staci Webber had told her to read about.

ജ)രു

When Monday morning arrived, Mary Jane informed Jack she would stay home as he expected her to but would make an appointment with a psychiatrist outside the prison. She preferred keeping her private business out of the workplace. Jack fully understood and agreed. An appointment was made for that Thursday. She had several days to rest and relax before her appointment. But instead of relaxing, she spent each day searching for answers in the Bible and on the Internet. Most of the information was found in the last book, Revelations—the book she always thought of as a very mysterious book written in riddles.

She read about how one of the mightiest angels of Heaven threw Lucifer into the bottomless pit and bound him with a great chain for 1000 years. And, one day, when he is released, he will appear on earth as God. He will fool everyone with signs and miracles, even Christians. Then, he will bring peace to the whole world. Next, she read of all the plagues that mankind would endure. She read of winged lions with many heads and about scrolls and seals. It was all very confusing to Mary Jane, even though she had read it several times before. Finally, after becoming overwhelmed, Mary Jane closed the book. It was just too difficult to figure out.

Thursday arrived, and she went to see the psychiatrist. She was very uncomfortable confiding in a stranger but told her everything. The psychiatrist diagnosed Mary Jane with hallucinations caused by Demonophobia, the fear of demons. She said the illness could have stemmed from witnessing Staci Webber's execution, working in the prison with people that had committed evil crimes, Jack's hospital experience, or a combination of all these experiences. Time off from work, anti-anxiety medication, and group sessions were suggested by the doctor.

"You're not alone. Not sure what's triggering it all, but in the last six months, I've diagnosed more patients with Demonophobia than ever before. In fact, we have a group session geared just for Demonophobia. We meet here every Monday afternoon. I offer cognitive behavioral therapy which helps teach you how to confront the fear and retrain yourself, so it doesn't control your life. Would you be interested?" asked the psychiatrist.

Quickly considering, Mary Jane accepted, and her first session with the psychiatrist ended. A prescription for Clonazepam, an anti-anxiety medication, was given to her, which she filled on the way home.

That evening, as she and Jack sat on the couch, she told him all about her appointment and took one of the Clonazepam pills. As they watched the 10 o'clock news broadcast, Mary Jane heard the phone ring. The kitchen phone was the closest. As Mary Jane got up from the couch, Jack watched her. "Where are you going?" he asked.

Awkwardly, she looked at him and responded, "To answer the phone."

"Hello," she answered. As Jack continued watching her, he witnessed her expression instantly change from relaxed to frantic. She roughly slammed the receiver down.

"What happened, Mary Jane?" asked Jack.

"It was her. It was Staci Webber," she nervously answered as she stood there, staring at the phone.

"Mary Jane, the phone didn't ring. Maybe it's your new medication."

"Jack, I clearly heard it ring and clearly heard her voice. Maybe you just didn't hear it," she defiantly claimed.

Acknowledging her distress, he didn't want to aggravate her and calmly urged her back to the couch.

"Maybe I didn't. Come back and sit with me."

"No, you don't believe me. I can tell. I'm going to bed. The Clonazepam's making me sleepy anyway."

"Okay, do you want me to come with you?"

"No, go ahead and watch the news. I'm going to read a little and try to relax."

As she lay down on the comfortable bed, she tried to concentrate on her breathing—tried to slow it down. She didn't want Jack to know how stressed she was. She wondered if the phone really hadn't rung, and became even more worried about herself. She knew that Jack was probably correct. After all, it was she that was seeing a psychiatrist, not he. Reading may help, she thought and picked the Bible up which was on her nightstand. She flipped it open to a delicate blue bookmark in the book of 1 Peter. Sometime before, she had highlighted a passage, and her eyes fell directly on it. 1 Peter 5:8 read,

> Be sober, be watchful: your adversary the devil, as a roaring lion, walks about, seeking whom he may devour.

She read no further for she got stuck on that one verse. She wondered if there were any hidden clues or knowledge in the passage, other than the obvious. She became obsessed with the verse and picked it apart, studying it word for word.

First, she looked into the lion kingdom. Why was a lion used and not a bear or any other ferocious hunter? And, why would the lion be roaring?

She retrieved her iPad and began her study. As Mary Jane read about lions in the wild, she learned that when they are not just hungry, but ravenously hungry, they roar. With that information, in her mind, she pictured a devil, roaming the earth, roaring—roaring because he was ravenously hungry—for human destruction.

She also learned that lions are not the fastest hunter in the wild, but the animals they hunt are some of the fastest on earth. So, the lion must hide and patiently wait for a sign of weakness. Once it detects the weakness, it waits for the right moment to spring from its hiding place and onto the unsuspecting prey.

The lion preys on the weak—the young, the old, the sick, and the ones not being vigilant, the ones that are not on the lookout, the ones not paying attention.

"So, the devil and his comrades, like the lion, are ravenously hungry—starving and hiding right next to us, patiently watching our every move, ready to pounce on us at the first sign of weakness," she concluded.

❧ ☙

That night in her dreams, a winged lion hovered over the earth, roaring with mouth wide open and its head quickly thrashing back and forth while on patrol. Its teeth were jagged and covered in blood from its last victim. Its bloodshot, angry eyes were darting to and fro, seeking its next meal with an insatiable appetite. Mary Jane looked on as the beast began to fly back and forth. It dove down in a fast spiral, just like a seabird, and snatched up an elderly man. As the elderly man screamed and kicked from within the jaws of the beast, the beast flew back up into the air. Once back up, the beast crunched the old man's body in its powerful jaw. Blood gushed out of winged lion's mouth and rained back down onto the earth. Even though Mary Jane no longer wanted to witness the slaughter, the dream continued on anyway. She helplessly watched as the beast stopped in mid-air and spread its wings. From the slimy pores of its haunches, came many smaller but identical creatures, which did exactly as it did. Then there were millions of them zigzagging to and fro all over the earth. There were so many that they bumped into one another. Below, on the earth, no one saw them flying above. Everyone was going about their daily lives, completely ignorant of the dangers lurking above them. Finally, Mary Jane saw the reason they could not see. The people on the earth had no eyes—only empty, dark eye sockets. The blind, easy prey was plentiful.

౷౸౿

Her dreams and her newfound knowledge haunted her every day. She began following the instructions of the verse, 1 Peter 5:8, and tried to stay vigilant and observant. She met others in the group sessions that were having the same dreams and fears that she was having. She and the rest of the group felt that they possessed a knowledge that others had not been given.

Everyone, not of the support group, that knew Mary Jane, helplessly watched her transformation. Her parents, Jack, her psychiatrist, and her friends had no idea how to help Mary Jane. In return, Mary Jane had no idea how to help them. She tried explaining the dangers to all of them, but they could not comprehend.

"They are like the blind people of my dreams," she told herself.

Chapter 14
The Mark?

Two months passed, and Jack remembered Mary Jane as she was before and still deeply loved her. He waited for her patiently, hoping that she would, one day, return to her former self. Mary Jane stayed at home most of the time. Rarely, she left. When she did, it was either to her parents' house or to see the psychiatrist.

One morning, after Jack had gone to work, Mary Jane sat on the couch to watch the morning news. The pretty blond news reporter said with an informing expression,

We have an exciting new electronic device to tell you about called an RFID, which stands for radio frequency identification. It is a microchip about the size of a grain of rice. It was recently approved by the FDA and is now being implemented into employees of three Fortune 100 companies.

These tiny little chips are causing quite a stir due to the fact that they are being implanted into human subjects. As of now, the selected implant site is the right hand. Apparently, it's a quick and practically painless procedure. A surgeon uses a local anesthetic to deaden the hand and a syringe to inject the device.

So far, these microchips are only being used as an access device. For example, they allow these Fortune 100 company employees access to enter the building, the computers, the copiers, lockers, and even the bathrooms with a simple wave of the hand. Many say they hold the key to the future. Everything about you can be saved on these remarkable tiny chips—everything from your social security number to your health records. Imagine, going to the doctor and not having to fill out a stack of paperwork. The medical facility would simply swipe your hand with an electronic scanner, similar to the ones used to check you out at the grocery store. Instantly and conveniently, they would have access to all of your needed information.

Causing the biggest controversy of all is the ability of these little chips to conduct all financial transactions. Many say that Big Brother will have too much access into everyone's life. But still, others are very excited about the financial freedom these chips can bring. For instance, no more waiting in line to deposit or withdraw money from financial institutions. No more credit cards, driver's license, social security cards, passports, or any other form of identification. Every single detail about a person can be accessed through the RFID.

The maiden voyage of these microchips was initiated this past Monday. The implantation of the device was made mandatory at the three companies. Employees had a choice to accept or decline. But if they decline, they forfeit their position in the company—and many did just that. So far 1,200 employees have resigned from their jobs due to this new technology.

The news reporter continued, but Mary Jane could no longer hear the words that she was saying.

"Oh, my God! I was wrong. We are living in the days Revelation speaks of. It said it would come swiftly like a thief in the night. This is the beginning of the end," Mary Jane said as she looked down rubbing her forehead. The phone rang out breaking her concentration.

"Hello," she answered.

"Hi, Sweetie. How's it going?" Jack asked.

"Well, I just saw a very disturbing news broadcast," she explained.

"What was it about?" he asked.

"About a microchip they are implanting into people. It sounds like, before long, everyone will have them and all of our personal information will be on them."

"Oh, yeah, we actually had a meeting a couple weeks back about implementing them here at the prison," Jack nonchalantly said.

"What? You never said anything about that to me. Why didn't you tell me about that?" Mary Jane squealed.

"Easy! It's not that big of a deal. It's no different than having a driver's license or a social security card or a key, for that matter," he said trying to sound unbiased. Secretly, he realized that he hadn't told her because he knew what her reaction would be. After all, she already had problems that she was dealing with, and he didn't want to add to them.

"Don't you know this could be the mark of the beast that the Bible warned us about?" Mary Jane inquired.

"No, Mary Jane. I don't think that at all. The Bible says that the mark of the beast is the name of the Antichrist or his number which is 666. This is neither. It's simply an electronic source of identification," he protested.

"Don't you think it to be odd that they are implanting them in the right hand, one of the places the Bible says the mark of the beast will be?" she asked.

Chuckling, he said, "Not really. That's coincidental."

Mary Jane was insulted by Jack's laughter and helplessly stopped trying to convince him about the matter.

Several weeks passed, and Jack realized he could no longer keep the new prison policy a secret from Mary Jane. He knew exactly how she would react. She would refuse and lose her position. He decided to tell her Monday after he got home from work. He never did like Mondays and decided if the evening was going to be ruined by the news, it might as well be done on the worst day of the week.

Jack didn't know how to be coy. Normally, he just spoke his mind but was now trying to figure out how to delicately break the news to Mary Jane. Eventually, he came to the conclusion that there wasn't a delicate way to break it to her.

So, when Monday evening arrived, he did just that.

"Mary Jane, I need to talk to you about something," he said over dinner.

"God! That doesn't sound good," she responded.

"Well, it's really all in how you take it. Honestly, I don't think it's bad. But you, on the other hand, might."

"Don't keep me in suspense. What?"

"The prison system is going to be the first of all government entities to try out the new microchips."

"What? When does it start?"

"They have already microchipped most of the prisoners, and they have given all employees one month to comply."

Jack watched as Mary Jane turned white as a ghost as she quickly arose from the dinner table. Instantaneously, Jack also stood and helped her to the couch.

"I know what you're thinking, Mary Jane. It's not the mark."

"Are you planning on getting it?" she asked.

"If I want to keep my job, I have to."

"You can't. You will burn in hell for all eternity if you do."

"Mary Jane, if I thought it had anything to do with the end of time prophecy, I wouldn't. But it's nothing like that."

With strong conviction, she said, "Oh, my God! Don't you remember that the Bible says many will be fooled? You are being fooled, Jack. You better read Revelations again and think about this real hard before you do something that's going to send you into eternal damnation."

"What would you have me do, Mary Jane? I've worked there for a long, long time. I probably couldn't get a job doing anything else—and definitely couldn't make the kind of money that I do. What would we do with no money? Are you ready to give up food and shelter and go live in the mountains?" he forcefully protested.

Mary Jane didn't know what to say. She threw her hands up and walked away. She had to get away from the conversation and from Jack, for then. She walked out of the front door and started walking down the street. All of a sudden, she wanted to go home—home to Alvin.

After Mary Jane's walk, she explained to Jack that she was going home for a couple of days. Jack couldn't help but feel that he was losing Mary Jane. Maybe, he thought, he had been a little rough.

Mary Jane didn't waste any time packing. Within an hour, she had a bag packed. Jack carried her bag and helped her into the car.

Goodbye kisses and I love you's were ritually completed. But Jack wasn't feeling any warmth coming from Mary Jane. Jack watched as she drove away. He went back inside and wept for the first time in a long time. "This is why I didn't let anyone get into my heart," he said to an empty house.

On the way to Alvin, Mary Jane thought of all the friends she had made at the prison—Isabella, Officer Dave, and a countless number of others.

She wondered, would they get the mark? How many of them will be fooled? How many of them don't even know about the mark? She wished she could save them, but knew she couldn't. She couldn't even convince Jack.

ഇ൫

Jack called Mary Jane several times a day. Lovingly, they spoke with each other. Jack, once again, started to feel that Mary Jane did still love him. Mary Jane did still love Jack, but she knew she must place her focus on survival without the mark. She decided to prepare for complete self-reliance. She hoped it wouldn't come to that, but if it did, she planned on being ready. She started gathering seeds of as many vegetables as she could and convinced her parents to buy more fruit trees. She bought elderberry bushes for immune support.

For a long time, her parents had talked about getting chickens so they could have fresh eggs. So, she easily talked them into building a chicken yard and buying some baby chicks. She also had her father check the generator to make sure it was operating properly. Her parents had a water well, but she wasn't sure how to get water out of it if there was no electricity to run the pump. So, she logged onto her Amazon account and ordered several survival books. Her parents noticed everything she was doing and asked why. She didn't want to alarm them but told them about how the prison microchipped all the prisoners and would soon microchip all the employees. Confiding in them, she explained her fears that the microchip might be the mark of the beast. They were Christians and believed Mary Jane might have a point. But even more so, they didn't trust the government. They had watched, as they aged, the government take more and more control away from them. They knew the government was slowly taking freedom away because if they did it too quickly, people would fight back.

"That's what they do, Mary Jane. They get their foot in the door. Then, they move on to invading the whole house—one room at a time," Earl chimed in.

"They're sneaky bastards, too. They didn't let this out to the public. Me and Mama wouldn't even know if you wouldn't have told us. I haven't seen anything about this on the news," he continued.

That evening, after dinner, Mary Jane and her parents sat down to watch the evening news together.

"They're in complete control of what comes out of that box," stated Earl. "My father and all his fallen comrades would roll over in their graves if they knew what the hell was going on here. I tell ya, it's a slap in the face to all of us who fought and died for freedom," Earl said with teary eyes. "But I'm a believer. I knew it would come one day. Just didn't believe it was gonna be in our time," he said trying to gain composure.

"Okay, Earl. Let's listen and see if they tell us anything we ought to know," said Marjorie as she watched the reporter.

History has taught us that using religion can bring peace and bridge gaps between nations. Early in the 1980's, Cardinal Antonio Samoré, supported by the Catholic Church, helped settle discontent between Chile and Argentina. Also in the 1980's, Pope John Paul II influentially helped topple communist regimes. And, more recently, Pope Alexis, in the name of peace, welcomed both Israel and

Palestinian presidents to the Vatican for an evening of prayers. Prayers of peace were issued by all in attendance. Today, we bring you the sad news that Pope Alexis has announced that he will step down from the papacy due to health reasons.

This event has led many to wonder who the new pope will be. Rumor has it, that one cardinal, in particular, Peter Alaricus, is being highly considered. Appealing to many Catholics, the cardinal is very dedicated to restoring peace in the Middle East. He plans on building, what he terms, A Temple of Peace on the Temple Mount in Jerusalem. Of course, the Palestinians and the Israelites alike are warning against this measure. Tomorrow, we will continue this coverage and explain why this is causing such an uproar in Jerusalem.

"That's an easy one. Any fool should know why that would cause an uproar," stated Earl.

"Why?" asked Marjorie.

"I'll tell y'all when we have plenty of time. It's a story that spans over four thousand years. It started when God promised Abraham and his descendants a new home in Canaan which is now known as Israel."

"I know you're long winded Dad, but can't you summarize it for us?" pleaded Mary Jane.

"You want me to summarize over four thousand years?" Earl asked with a grin.

"Yes, please! I want to know. With everything else going on, I know it has to tie in somehow," stated Mary Jane.

"It probably does. Okay, I'll give it a try. I guess the best way would be to start from the beginning. Keep in mind; I'm summarizing and leaving out a whole lot of details."

"Okay," agreed Mary Jane and Marjorie, both wide-eyed with anticipation. They both knew Earl was a whiz at history and loved to hear him tell it.

"As I said, God told Abraham, a Jew, to leave his homeland and journey to a land flowing with milk and honey, the land known at that time as Canaan. So, he did. And, ever since he arrived on that Promised Land, he and his descendants have had to fight and die for it. One of his descendants, King Solomon, built a temple known as the Holy Temple on the Temple Mount, also known as Mount Zion. You probably know that Solomon was known for his Godly wisdom, and even more so, for his riches. He was so rich that he used tons of pure gold and silver to build this temple and dedicated it to honor God. Then, the Romans came along and destroyed it somewhere around 580 B.C. And, of course, they seized all of the gold and riches from the temple and the surrounding city.

"The defeated descendants of Abraham were then transferred to Babylon. After some time, the Jews were allowed to return to their homeland but were still under Roman control. After they returned, the second temple was built on the exact site as the first. But this time, the temple took over 500 years to build. Herod the Great was the one that is given credit for enlarging and completing the second temple. It was enormous. It was 144,000 square meters—about the size of twenty football fields. After it was completed, there was a great revolt. The Jews finally had enough and revolted against the Romans, who still had control over them. The Romans, in return, destroyed and looted the city and the temple for a second time. The temple wasn't rebuilt after that. Just as well, because, shortly after the Jews recovered Jerusalem, the Arabs conquered them in 638 A.D. Then the Arabs built a dome on the Temple Mount. The Arabs are Muslims, and according to their belief, that spot—the Temple Mount—is where the prophet Mohamed ascended into Heaven. So it is a very sacred place to them, as well.

"Then came The Great Crusades. The Crusaders, a.k.a. the Catholics, turned the temple into a church, erecting a cross on the dome. Then they—the crusaders—were driven out. And sometime after the fourteenth century, the Temple Mount became a major Muslim prayer site.

"More recently, in 1967, Israel took back the eastern part of Israel and the Temple Mount. For the first time in over 2000 years, the Jewish people had access to what they called "the Old City."

"But to avoid a holy war with the Muslims, Israel allowed for the inclusion of both religions at the temple. That's why there is so much friction over there. The Israelites have to staff thousands of police to limit the number of men and age of men allowed at the Temple Mount at any one time. Since the two opposing religions share the site, very often, fighting between the two occur. It's bad enough that two religions are trying to share the same site, but to each religion, the site holds very special religious meaning. Throw a third religion into the competition, Catholicism, and there is going to be a holy war," he ended with a big sigh.

"But what about the Antichrist? I thought he would appear on the scene after the third temple was built," inquired Mary Jane.

"Yes, he is. I've done many studies on the Antichrist. I've read several different views about who he will be. Interestingly, one view says he will be a pope. And, that's the one I believe to be correct, especially now, after seeing that news broadcast. I'll tell you why. Until now, no one could fathom how a third temple could be erected on the Mount, seeing how the two religions share the site. Everyone knows that, if either tries to erect a temple, the other will immediately wage war. Neither side seems to want that. There is a verse in Daniel that says the Antichrist will negotiate peace between the Jews and the Arabs. I ask you, who else has that power?" Earl asked.

"No way! I can't see that a man of faith would be the Antichrist," smirked Mary Jane.

"The Catholics aren't as faithful as you may think. Do you know the pope's hat, or mitre, has the Latin words, 'Vicarious Filii Dei' inscribed on it?" asked Earl.

"No, so what does that mean?" asked Mary Jane.

"It's Latin, and it means, "substitution for the son of God." Look up the words in a Latin dictionary for yourself. I did.

Prophesy says that the Antichrist will sit in the temple and claim that he is God. That's exactly what they do already. And, did you know that the Catholics took the second commandment out of God's original Ten Commandments that were given to Moses?"

he went on.

"What?" Mary Jane asked with disbelief.

"That's right. Look it up. They took the second commandment out that says, "Thou shalt not make any graven image of anything on earth and not to bow down to any image, for I am a jealous God." Then, to make sure there were still ten commandments, they took the tenth one and divided it into two commandments—making it the ninth and tenth."

"Why would they do that?" asked Mary Jane.

"Many believe they descended from the scribes and Pharisees of the Bible. Don't you see how the church has tried to replace God? Catholics go to confession and ask for forgiveness from their so-called "father" as if he has the power to forgive them of their sins. That is a lie of the devil. The only one that can forgive you of your sins is God himself. Besides all that, it says in Revelations that the Antichrist will be a descendant of the people that destroyed the first Holy Temple. The people that destroyed the temple are the Romans. Maybe I, with a lot of others, are wrong, but there sure are a lot of reasons that the Antichrist may come from them. Actually, even they themselves have prophesied that an evil pope will one day arrive on the scene. Have you heard the theory of "the last pope"?

"No, but do tell," Mary Jane said with a little more interest.

"Apparently, St. Malachy, an Irish archbishop, had a vision in 1139. In this vision, he saw that there would be 112 more popes before judgment day. Also, Martin Luther, along with countless other religious leaders down through history believe that the Antichrist will be a pope. Research everything I've told you and see what you find for yourself. Oh, one more thing: the word 'pope' is Latin for 'papa' or 'father.' They are plainly claiming to be the father. In my opinion, that's pure blasphemy."

"Summarizing isn't one of your best qualities," laughed Mary Jane.

She just couldn't accept that the Antichrist could possibly be a pope. She thought well of the Catholic popes for trying to create peace. Besides, she had seen evil people with their cold, dead fish eyes, and not one of the popes possessed those eyes. Their conversation ended as Mary Jane and her mother started cleaning off the dinner table. Earl just shrugged his shoulders and thought to himself, *Many will be deceived.*

As Mary Jane helped her mom wash the dishes, she heard her cell phone ring from the living room.

"I'll be right back, Mom," declared Mary Jane.

"I can finish. You go ahead," answered Marjorie.

Marjorie was so glad Mary Jane had found a good boyfriend. For a long time, Marjorie had prayed she would. Since Mary Jane seemed so satisfied with Jack, Marjorie had moved on to praying that Mary Jane would marry Jack and give her grandchildren.

Marjorie turned the water off so that she could eavesdrop on Mary Jane's telephone conversation with Jack.

"How was your day?" she heard Mary Jane ask from the living room.

"What do you mean by interesting?" suspiciously asked Mary Jane.

"So, regardless of what I wanted, you did it anyway?" boldly stated Mary Jane.

Marjorie whispered to herself, "Uh oh!"

Mary Jane argued, "I hope, for your sake, that I'm wrong, and it's not the mark of the beast."

"What in God's name is she talking about?" Marjorie wondered out loud.

Epilogue

Meanwhile, Epic soared over the waters of the Atlantic and then over the Caribbean. He considered the sun-kissed people of Belize but departed that region for a land full of easy opportunity.

A Note from the Author

If you find it as fascinating as I do that fallen angels may have borne children with earthly women, start your research with Genesis 6:1-2.

Then, begin an Internet search of the Nephilim, which were the offspring of the fallen angels.

Also, read the book of Enoch. Enoch was one of two people in the Bible that were taken up to heaven without dying. You can find an account of this in Genesis 5:24. Why was his book left out of the Bible?

If you read Enoch, you'll discover something else you may never have heard. You'll read Enoch's version of why God flooded the earth. I'll give you a hint: It has something to do with the Nephilim.

The Mark of the Beast
Sneak Peak of Book 2
Reign of the Antichrist

Breaking news! We will return to the regular schedule after this breaking news report. It has been reported that two Uranium enrichment plants in Natanz and Qom have just been attacked. No claims have been made as of yet, but it is believed that Israel launched the military strike. For quite some time, the UN has stated that Israel has legal justification for war against Iran, given Iran's constant threats to destroy the Jewish state. It appears that Israel has decided to act upon this legal justification...